17816

Fic
Ban

D1109671

RL= 5.0
pts = 9.0

One More River

LYNNE REID BANKS

REVISED EDITION

Morrow Junior Books

NEW YORK

For Gladys Richards,
who chose to stay
and share our war

ACKNOWLEDGMENTS My grateful thanks are due to Hana Raz; Tamar Sachs; and my husband, Chaim Stephenson, who have all helped me with the background of this book. Also to Tirza Lavi for allowing me to use her poem which appears on pages 201–203.

A glossary of Hebrew (and Yiddish) words and terms used in this story will be found on pages 245–248.

AUTHOR'S NOTE This book is fictional. The characters, the story, and the kibbutz are all imaginary. The historical facts alone are true.

Book design by Karen Palinko

Printed in the United States of America.

1 2 3 4 5 6 7 8 9 10

Library of Congress Cataloging-in-Publication Data
Reid Banks, Lynne, 1929–
One more river / Lynne Reid Banks.—Rev. ed.
p.   cm.
Summary: Fourteen-year-old Lesley is upset when her parents
abandon their comfortable life in Canada for a kibbutz in Israel
prior to the 1967 war.
ISBN 0-688-10893-8 (trade)
[1. Jews—Fiction.   2. Kibbutzim—Fiction.   3. Israel-Arab War,
1967—Fiction.]   I. Title
PZ7.R27370n   1992
[Fic]—dc20   91–43152   CIP   AC

Contents

One more river,
And that's the river of Jordan.
One more river,
There's one more river to cross.

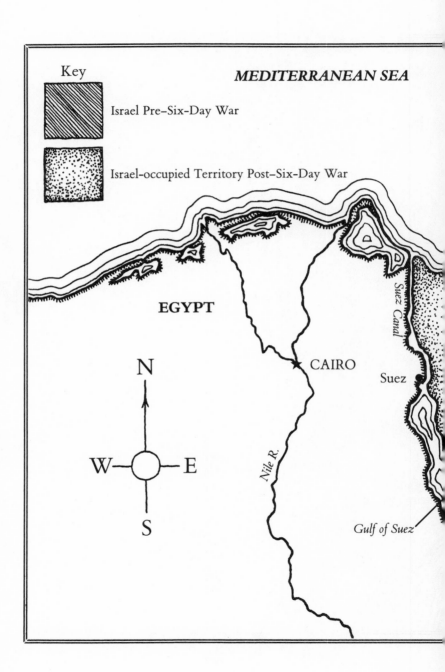

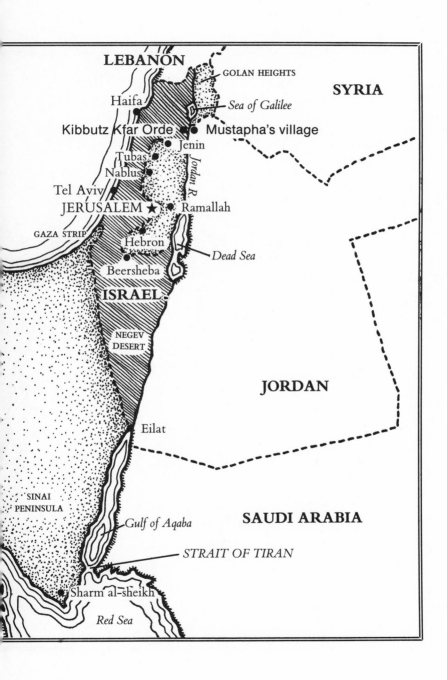

O N E

A Terrible Announcement

It wouldn't have been so bad if Lesley had had any warning. Or rather, if she'd heeded the warning signs.

She had to admit, long afterward, that there had been some. She'd just ignored them. Life was so exciting and full at the time that any shadow that fell on her, any suspicion of a shadow even, she simply darted out from under and danced blithely on her way as if it weren't there. She wasn't prepared to admit that anything could go wrong, that anything could ever change.

The shadow, such as it was, was in her parents' manner.

Lesley loved both her parents, though some

1

doubts occasionally crossed her mind about her father. He was always lovely to *her,* and to her mother; in addition, he was handsome, successful, and generous. But Lesley could never quite forget that awful business about her brother, Noah—she'd never understood about that.

Noah was much older than she was—eight years—but a brother was a brother. To exile him from the family, to never speak about him, because of religion . . . Well, of course they were an Orthodox family, they kept kosher and went to synagogue and so on, and she knew her parents felt very strongly Jewish. Still, it didn't fully make sense to Lesley, and it couldn't help seeming to her some-times as if her father had behaved—not very well about it.

But that was a long time ago. Three years now . . . She'd been told to forget about it, and if she hadn't, quite, it was only because nobody had really explained it all to her, so it nagged at her mind like a locked door.

Aside from that, life was good, it was almost one hundred percent perfect as a matter of fact, what with having rich parents, being nice-looking (most people said), well up on schoolwork, good at sports, and now having the most exciting boyfriend in the entire eighth grade. She was comfortably aware that she was envied, but that didn't really affect her popularity. What more could anyone want?

So the funny atmosphere at home—the little glances, the conversations that stopped as she came into a room, the talk she could just hear through her bedroom floor long after she'd gone to bed instead of the friendly sounds of televi-sion—none of these really impinged on her happiness and her confidence that life in general was great, and would go on being great forever.

One bright, crunchy September day, the sort of prairie fall day that always made her feel her very best, Lesley came home from school a little later than usual, having stopped off at her friend Sonia's for a bacon sandwich and a good old gossip.

All the talk was about the junior Thanksgiving dance in early October. Happily, they'd both been invited in good time. Sonia's partner was in ninth grade, a grade ahead of the girls, and this made her, for once, more envied than Lesley, but Lesley liked her enough not to mind.

Anyway, she had Lee. He was just too wonderful. Tall, handsome, a basketball star, hot stuff in the drama club—everything. He was also Jewish, which meant no objections from her parents. He and she had swapped class rings to show they were going steady. And now all she could think about—apart from who was going with whom to the dance—was her trip to the store on Saturday with her mother, to pick out a really gorgeous dress for the occasion.

"I wonder if they've got a strapless one in *midnight blue* satin?" she'd said dreamily. "Lee likes me in blue, he says I've got blue lights in my hair."

"You're so lucky!" Sonia had said (she was always saying it). "Your dad *owning* Shelby's! I can't imagine just being able to walk into the Junior Miss department and pick out the shooshiest gown in the place and say, 'That one!' and not even have your mom look at the price tag."

"Yeah, it's nice," said Lesley. She didn't know she

sounded smug. Her father owning the best store in town was part of what made life good, but she was also used to it. It had always been the same, from the time when it was the *toy* department she could pick things from.

Before she'd left Sonia's, she'd gone to the bathroom and gargled with some undiluted Listerine. Disgusting taste!—but she couldn't risk either of her parents smelling the bacon on her breath. Bacon wasn't kosher, especially not with a glass of milk! She washed the slight guilt away with the grease, said so long and see you tomorrow to Sonia, and walked home through the familiar streets with her schoolbag over her shoulder, full of dreams of a long, low-cut blue satin dress that set off her hair and her newly developed figure.

Her father was home—his car was in the drive. She peered in through the front window with the ruched curtains into the big, elegant living room. Yes, there he was, and there was her mother, too, talking as usual. . . . She tapped on the window.

They both jumped and their heads snapped around. It flashed through Lesley's mind that if they'd knocked on Sonia's window while Lesley had been eating the bacon sandwich, she'd have jumped just like that. What were they up to?

The shadow came close suddenly. But she ducked out from under it and ran up the wide front steps. She didn't know the shadow was following her and that this time she couldn't escape it.

As she let herself in through the gleaming white front door, her father appeared in the double doors of the living room. He wasn't tall like Lee's father. He was short and stocky, but strong-looking, though recently he had put on some weight. He had a full head of gray, curly hair that Lesley loved to play with. He was always immaculately dressed and polished his shoes—very good ones—every single night. That used to be Noah's job, Lesley suddenly remembered, a second before it registered that her father was not smiling his invariable welcome-home smile.

"Come in here, Les, will you? We want to talk to you."

She dismissed the shadow. Talk to her? Why not? She bounced into the living room and parked herself on the wide, brocaded arm of the chair he'd been sitting in.

"Hi, Mom! Am I about to be let in on the secret?" she asked perkily.

Her mother jumped again—well, her eyes did. "Secret?"

"Sure! I knew you'd tell me when you were ready."

Her parents exchanged one of those funny looks, and she knew she'd hit it right. She felt rather pleased at having been smarter than they thought. But that feeling gave way almost at once to unease because neither of them looked as if the secret were a nice one.

Her father sat down in the chair beside her. She put her arm around his shoulders and started to play with his hair, but he said, "Les, will you sit over there, please, where I can see you?"

Chilled, she moved. Her father was looking at her very seriously. Her mother was smiling, but nervously—she put her finger into her mouth very daintily and bit on a hangnail.

"Is it something I've done?" Lesley asked, the bacon sandwich lurking in her conscience.

"No, no," they both said at once. And her father said, "It's something we're all going to do."

"Something tremendously exciting!" said her mother brightly.

Ah! Now Lesley knew. It was about Christmas. At last they'd seen sense! Lee's family went skiing in the Rockies every year at a Jewish resort, and for them there were no problems about parties and a tree and carol-singing and all the stuff Jews weren't supposed to do but that, if you stayed home, it was impossible to keep the rules about. Lesley had been hinting for months. She jumped up and let out a yell of happiness.

"We're going to go skiing!" she cried, clapping her hands.

"We're going to emigrate," said her father.

There was a brief pause. The words dropped into Lesley's mind innocently, like any other words, and there exploded like a bomb. Every muscle in her face went slack. Her arms fell to her sides. Everything in the room shrank away for a second and then came rushing back as if to crush her.

Her eyes went to her mother. She would take it back—she must. Because emigrating meant leaving Canada. Permanently. And that couldn't be true. It couldn't be what her father had said, or meant.

But her mother was nodding. Nodding and smiling like a doll. *Yes* she was nodding, as if it were quite possible and reasonable, yes. But it must be no. No. No. It *must* be.

Lesley felt the shadow falling around her like a heavy canvas, but she fought it off.

6

"What do you mean?" she said without raising her voice, though she was almost screaming inside.

"Sit down, Lesley, and listen to what I'm going to tell you."

Something went flash in Lesley's head. This had happened before. It had happened three years ago when her father had told her that Noah was disgraced, that he had left their faith, and that he wasn't part of them anymore. *Part of us . . . He's not part of us.* The words came back.

But what were *they* part of? What was her father tearing to bits now?

She found herself sitting in the big chair, clinging to its arms. Her eyes were fixed on her father and the shadow was all around her so that she could hardly see him.

"We're Jews," he said (and this, too, was like that other time). "And we're Canadians. It's becoming harder and harder to remember which comes first. My father knew, because he came from the Old Country. And your grandmother"—he nodded toward Lesley's mother—"she was first-generation, too. She knew. They brought us up to know that the most important thing for a Jew is to survive *as a Jew.* To keep faith with the past."

Lesley began to pant. What was he talking about?

"But Mom keeps kosher," she gasped. "We go to *shul.* And you're forever telling me—"

"Jewishness isn't a matter of what you're told. It's in your blood and bones. If we were doing our job right as Jewish parents, you'd be incapable of doing . . . a lot of the things we know very well you do."

"Just because I sometimes eat—"

7

Her father cut in swiftly. "It's got very little to do with what you eat. Kosher's not the real point at all. Keeping kosher is just a symbol, sometimes of something Jews forget to feel—Jews like us who live in other people's countries."

Other people's countries?

"But isn't Canada our country?"

"No. Not really."

"Why not? *Why not?*"

"It's a Christian country."

There was a moment's silence. Then Lesley burst out, "But there aren't any Jewish countries! Except . . ."

"Except Israel. Exactly. And that's where we're going."

Lesley simply couldn't take it in at first. Israel!

Suddenly her mind began to thaw out of its shock and look at this—could it be a *fact*? Could her father, whom she'd always loved and trusted, really be going to uproot them all from their safe, comfortable, happy life, and drag them off to that faraway place where there was always trouble and fighting?

"But—but—I was *born* here! It's my *home!*" she burst out. Her voice wasn't quiet now. "You can't expect me to leave—my house, my street, school—all my friends—Sonia—Lee—"

Each word took her deeper into strange, untrodden realms of despair, and she began to cry, her voice rising and rising. Her father stood up and came toward her, but she dodged him and ran away to the window.

Through it she could see the garden, with its beautiful fiery maple tree, the hedge she used to hide behind for fun when her father came home, the trim lawn where the couples had danced and necked on her fourteenth birthday, just a month ago. . . . Two of her friends came down the street as she stared through a blur of tears, riding their bikes and laughing. . . . Safe.

And beyond, the Saskatchewan River, her river that she had played by and looked at and loved and taken for granted all her life, gliding by in the sun as if nothing were happening.

She whirled around and faced her parents. Her face was contorted.

"I'll die if you make me go!" she shouted. "You can't do this to people!" And when her father reached toward her, she struck down his arm. "I don't want to be a Jew if this is what it means. I'm Canadian, do you hear me? I'm *Canadian!*"

"And part of you will always——" began her mother's voice soothingly in the background, but her father cut in.

"It's better if you look ahead now. Our future isn't here. It's in a place where we can be ourselves without fear or favor. We're going to Israel, Lesley. Accept it."

"I won't!" she screamed passionately. "I won't, I won't, I won't!" She heard how it sounded, like a spoiled baby throwing a tantrum, and she saw her mother jump up, but she was beyond control.

A moment later, she was slamming the doors of the room so hard she felt the vibrations all the way up her arms to her shoulders. She left the front door swinging, ran across the main road without looking out for cars, and flung herself down the riverbank to her own secret place. There she fell to the ground and lay crying aloud with bitter incomprehension, rage, and fear.

The bright autumn leaves stuck in her hair as she twisted

her head back and forth. Below her, through the trees, the slow, majestic river glinted. Being near it had soothed and cheered her all her life. But now she wept on heedlessly, beyond comfort, as if the end of summer were the end of the world.

T W O

Rebellion

It was necessary to rebel. To fight it. Never to give in.

To accept it in any way at all would be treason to Canada, to everything she loved and belonged to. Her parents? She didn't belong to parents who could do this. She couldn't love them. They were her enemies. In that bad hour she lay on the riverbank, that was how she felt, and she was quite sure she would never feel differently.

She needed allies. So when she'd finished crying at last, feeling no better but simply out of tears, she tucked her shirt into her jeans, picked the leaves out of her hair, wiped her face with the palms of her hands, and climbed

11

back up to the road. She wanted Sonia. Sonia would understand and support her.

And so she did at first. Properly shocked by the sight of Lesley's dirty, tragic face, she pulled her upstairs to her bedroom, where she locked the door.

"What the heck's happened to you? You look a mess!"

"Daddy's gone mad. He's taking Mom and me to Israel."

"Israel! You mean, for a vacation?"

"No! He said we were emigrating."

"You mean, you'll be going forever?"

"Not if I can help it! First off, I'm going to try to stop them taking me there. They'll have to drag me. And if they do get me there, I'll run away, I'll find a way to come back."

Sonia stared at her with big, sad eyes.

"Do you really think you could—come back without them?"

Lesley swallowed and said nothing. It was a crazy dream, and she knew it.

Suddenly Sonia threw herself on her and hugged her.

"Gee, I'm gonna miss you!" she cried passionately, and burst into tears.

Although in a way this was exactly the reaction Lesley had wanted, in another way it irritated her. Sonia had accepted it straight away—she was almost kissing Lesley good-bye the minute she'd heard about it.

"I'm not going *tomorrow,*" she said rather crossly, disengaging herself from Sonia's arms.

"But I won't have a best friend anymore!" sobbed Sonia, throwing herself face down on the bed.

12

Lesley watched her. Sonia was in the school drama club, and now it occurred to Lesley that some part of her was rather enjoying this tragedy-queen bit. She felt Sonia was overdoing it.

"I'm the one that's going," Lesley said, handing Sonia a handful of tissues as a hint she should stop crying.

Sonia sat up and blew her nose. They were real tears. The sight of them consoled Lesley, until Sonia sniffed loudly and said, "Of course, you're lucky in a way."

"Lucky?"

"Well, I mean it's really *abroad,* isn't it?" she asked.

"Of course it's abroad," said Lesley impatiently.

"I mean not just the States or somewhere. It's the mystic East."

"It's not the 'mystic' East, it's the Middle East," Lesley said testily. "It's not India or China or somewhere. Don't you know where Israel is?"

"Yeah, sure. I guess . . . sort of. Anyhow, it sounds exciting."

"*Exciting!* It's just hot and dangerous and germy and stinky! And we don't even *have* to go there!"

"What do you mean?"

"I mean," said Lesley, trying to explain, "that if there was a pogrom here or something—"

"A what?"

"Don't you know what a pogrom is?"

"No?"

"It's—you know—when Jews were being killed in Russia."

"Well, how do you expect me to know that?"

"I thought everybody did," said Lesley, baffled. "If we

were being *driven out*, like my grandparents in Poland before the Second World War, I could understand it—if it was an enemy. But it's Daddy!"

"Yeah, it's tough. Gee, if my dad tried to . . . But there's a good side."

"Tell me one thing good! Just one!"

"Well, we can write to each other, I can tell you all the news about who's dating and stuff, and you can tell me what it's like there, and I'll read it out to the class. That'd be kind of fun."

Lesley stood up slowly. Her heart had gone cold.

"You know what's wrong with you," she said. "You have no imagination."

Sonia looked amazed. "Why are you acting so mean? I was only trying to make you feel better!"

"Don't you know I don't want to feel better?" Lesley shouted.

"You don't? Why not?"

"Oh . . . ! I can't explain and I shouldn't have to!"

And in a sudden burst of irrational fury, which later she would have great trouble excusing herself for, Lesley ran out of the room, down the stairs, and out, letting the screen door swing behind her.

So much for best friends, she fumed unreasonably. When the chips were down, when you really needed them, they just acted *crass*. Didn't know what a pogrom was! The "mystic East"! And probably couldn't even point to Israel on a map. Lesley tried to find the word for what Sonia was being, back there. Her father used it for people who had narrow outlooks. Provincial. That was it. . . .

Well, Lee was Jewish, he wouldn't be provincial, at least not about Israel!

She went straight to Lee's house. It was kind of a long walk and she nearly turned back twice, especially when she thought what she looked like. She was proud of her looks and never went to school or anywhere else without taking trouble. Now her dark hair hung in rattails and her face was probably dirty and her clothes certainly were, from lying on the riverbank. Well, but if he saw her like this he would be sure to feel shocked and sorry for her, and be on her side against her parents.

But it didn't work out like that.

He was shocked at first to see her in such a state. He even gave her a surreptitious hug, right there in his hall where his parents might see. His eyes were full of concern, which was warming. . . . But when she told him "Israel," everything changed.

"You're going there," he muttered, gazing at her in astonishment and—could it be? Could it possibly be— envy? He drew breath, took hold of her shoulders—and shook her.

"Lee! You're hurting!"

"I'm sorry! I'm just so—I wish I was you! You're so lucky! You're the luckiest person in the world!"

Him, too? "Are you crazy?" she asked incredulously.

"No, I'm not crazy. Just think of the adventure! It's what I've always wanted! To go out there, to be part of it . . . My folks never stop talking about it, oh yeah, red-hot Zionists the both of them, but when I say let's get up and *go* then, they always just smile at me as if I was stupid. They

15

like their comforts too much! They think our life is just the peaks. What else is there? Going to the office every day, playing stupid golf, playing *bridge,* watching TV, going shopping . . . *garbage.* Les, that's all they want."

"Lee—"

"But your dad . . . Wow. I always admired him, but now! Imagine, selling Shelby's, starting all over again—"

"Selling Shelby's!" That hadn't occurred to her.

"Well, he'll have to, won't he, you can't pack up a big department store into crates and ship it! What guts . . . gee . . . Wait till I tell my father—that's what I call *real* commitment, not just talking about it! And you!" He was gazing at her as if she'd just won a million dollars. "You'll grow up there, you'll speak the language, you'll be an Israeli! Say, Les, you'll be a soldier!" He gave her a bang on the back.

"A *soldier!*"

"Sure. All Israeli girls join the army unless they're married."

She stared at him. "You don't even care that I'm going!"

"Oh, baby, don't say that. I do." He gave her another hug, but there was too much exuberance in it and not nearly enough sadness. "Of course I do," he whispered. "But it can't be helped! We've got to be positive about it! Les, promise me you'll write. Tell me everything! You're great at writing. It'll be like being there myself."

"Is that all you can think of? What about . . ." But she couldn't say "us." She said, "What about the *dance?*"

"The what? Oh, that! Well, you'll still be here for that. But honest, Les, how can you even think about a silly junior hop when you're going to the greatest country in the world?"

16

Lesley didn't flounce out this time. She felt as if her insides were all hollow, as if her heart had gone out of her. She just said a very quiet good-bye to Lee and walked home slowly, slowly, feeling too tired to lift her feet properly.

There were to be no allies. She would have to fight on her own.

That night she locked herself in her room and wouldn't go down to supper. Her parents came and knocked on her door, and called her, and whispered together, and then left her. Her anger kept her staunch until they'd gone to bed. Then, and only then, she sneaked down and got herself something to eat.

She lay awake for hours, making plans. Next morning she again refused to come out.

"But, Lesley, what about school?" her mother wailed through the door.

"I won't go," she said between her teeth. "I'm staying home till—till you tell me *we're* staying home."

She heard her mother's footsteps retreating. First battle honors to her! But she didn't know how to take it from there. She couldn't live up in her room, creeping out like a mouse to eat when everyone was asleep. She'd die of boredom, for one thing.

She decided to wait till her father left for the store and then just stroll down to breakfast casually. She felt she could deal with her mother alone. It was her father she felt uncertain about, especially now. She'd seen something in his eyes yesterday when she'd started yelling that had scared her.

She waited and waited for him to leave. Her bedroom window overlooked the front drive. Nothing happened—he didn't come out; the garage doors stayed closed. She could hear the vacuum cleaner in the room below, and at last her hunger—her desire for normality—drove her to open her door and go quietly downstairs. She could snatch some food while her mother was in the living room and perhaps get back up unseen, if her dad was in his study. . . .

But he wasn't. He was sitting in the kitchen waiting for her.

She stopped dead in the doorway like a guilty criminal when she saw him, and then, furious with herself and with him, tossed her head and made for the fridge as if he weren't there.

"Lesley."

His voice was more forceful than she remembered it ever being. Instinctively she paused for a second, and then opened the fridge door. She had a glimpse of all the delicious foods that always filled it before it was slammed shut.

She whirled around, angry defiant words ready to throw at him, but that look was on his face again and the words froze in her mouth.

"I want to help you," he said. "We both do. Help you to come to terms with this. We know it's hard at first. But we can't help if you throw tantrums. Nor if you go on strike. You must not behave like a princess. I can't help you if you do. I can't *stand* you if you do."

The word "princess" had two meanings for Lesley. Her dad had often called her his little princess when she was younger. But now it meant something bad, something

18

other people said about rich Jewish girls. Just lately her dad had said, *Don't you ever turn into a "princess."* It meant spoiled. Pampered. No backbone. No character.

"I'm not a princess," she whispered. But she felt tears coming. She bit them back and threw up her head.

"You better not be, Lesley. Because where we're going, there'll be no room for J.A.P.s or J.C.P.s, either, I promise you." His hands crept to his waistline. "And no room for gone-to-seed old fat guys either. We're all going to have to change. Toughen up. Become *menschen.*"

"You're a *mensch,* aren't you, Daddy?" she said, trying to pacify him, trying to flatter him because she was frightened of him for the first time.

"Maybe I was once," he said. "Back at the beginning. I worked hard for everything I have. But those days are done. Now I'm just ticking over. I'm going soft. A man who depends on *golf* to keep his figure isn't a *mensch.* We've got it too easy. All of us."

"Is that why you're making us go? To make sure you're still a *mensch?*"

His eyes narrowed. His voice had a sharp edge to it as he said, "You're a smart girl, Les. Be smart enough not to get fresh with me. I'm doing this for all of us, but perhaps especially for you."

"You're doing this horrible thing for *me?*"

"Yes. I want you to grow up comfortable with your Jewishness, and I want you to grow up in a country where life is lived on an edge."

"What do you mean, an edge?"

"You'll see when we get there. Our life here is hollow.

It demands nothing. There are no true challenges. Without challenge we rot, mind, soul, and body."

Lesley stared at him blankly.

"Now then. Why aren't you in school?" he asked her sharply.

"I don't want to go."

"Your mother told me what you said. That's blackmail."

"You don't understand."

"No. It's you who don't understand. And you won't, not for some time yet. You just have to take what we're doing on trust."

"I can't!"

"You must. Certain things that come to us in life can't be fought. You just have to accept them, however hard they seem. Now, your mother and I have decided to emigrate. Perhaps we should have talked to you earlier, but we didn't want to get you upset before it was all decided. Finally. And it is, Les. Fixed. It is going to happen and nothing can stop it."

"Why not? If you changed your mind . . ."

"It's too late for that." He paused a moment and looked away. "I've sold the store."

The words had a ring of doom. Her father's voice was hollow as he spoke them.

Somehow Lesley found this almost harder to believe than the main news. Shelby's had been started by her grandfather as a little hat shop downtown. He'd built it up, and after he died, her father had taken it over, and built it up more, into the finest department store in town. It had been his life's work. It had been Lesley's pride, too. It had given her more than dresses and toys. It had given her her place in the world. "The Shelby girl . . ." Suddenly she felt she was a nobody.

"Why did you sell it, Daddy?" she wailed. "Why? It was our store, our family's—"

"No. It was mine. Nobody else ever worked in it, except your mother at the beginning."

"Noah—"

The word was not fully out of her mouth before her father turned on her.

"Quiet!"

He barked the word. His face was full of hard lines and cuts like scars. She saw he was middle-aged—suddenly. And it made her sorry for him, just for that moment, and out of that compassion came an insight—and a rash burst of courage.

"Is it because of him you're doing this? Because his name will never be on the store?"

He reached for her shoulders and, before she could dodge, had grasped them in furious hands and given her one hard shake. Then he let her go and turned away, stiff in every muscle.

"Not another word, Lesley. I beg of you. Not one more word on that subject. You understand now as much as you're old enough to understand. You can't control events. You can only face up to them. Like a *mensch,* or like a princess. I want a *mensch* for a daughter. Now go get your books and I'll drive you to school."

●   ●   ●

21

So ended Lesley's first rebel act. But it wasn't her last.

She thought about it and thought about it. In school she got some sympathy. Her teachers, when they heard, were very nice to her. They said they'd miss her, and she needed to hear that. The basketball team was full of dismay. Some of her friends said it was unfair and many added that *their* parents would never do anything so cruel. This strengthened her resolve not to go quietly.

At home she did as she was supposed to do. But she scarcely spoke. She knew, with one part of herself, that her parents considered she was sulking. *She* called it refusing to cooperate.

She showed not the slightest interest in the move. Once or twice her mother gently suggested that it would be good to read some books about Israel, or, even more important, try to study Hebrew in preparation for their new life. (Her favorite teacher suggested this, too.) She simply wouldn't listen. She turned her back—she turned her *mind*—completely away. Anything like that would be giving in, agreeing to go. They might force her, but she would never give her agreement to leaving her home.

In school they were studying the Reformation, and she learned how Luther, one of the founders of the Protestant Church, at the risk of his life stood before a Catholic court and said, "Here I stand. I can do no other." "It was a matter of principle," said the teacher approvingly. And something in Lesley sat up and said, "Yes!" She'd found the words to justify her attitude. She felt like a martyr.

In her thoughts, her father had become the bad guy in her life. The tyrant. The oppressor. This upset her deep down, but on the surface she was glad to have someone to fix her anger on. She wanted to go against him, do something that would express, to herself, her opposition to him. And one night when she was in her room, buried in a book, it came to her. Her great and dangerous rebel idea!

It came from four innocent little words in the book. "My brother and I . . ."

She had been told to forget her brother, but she hadn't. She couldn't. Now suddenly she became obsessed with him—but as more than just her lost brother: as a sort of weapon she could use against her father. She would find Noah, talk to him. It was the best way of defying her father that she could think of. Besides . . . Who knew? If best friends and boyfriends turn out no-go as allies, perhaps a brother might be better.

How to find him, though, was the next problem.

She racked her brains for several days, until at last she remembered something. At the time of the Great Row over Noah, she remembered hearing her Aunt Hannah— her mother's sister—shouting, "You're a pig-headed fanatic, Nat! You'll regret it to your last hour! Look around you. Times are changing. If you send your son to school with non-Jewish girls, what do you want from his life? Well, don't expect *me* to abide by this ban of yours. He'll need someone to turn to, poor boy!" And since then Auntie Hannah had only visited very occasionally, always when Lesley's father was not there.

Her phone number was in the back of her mother's engagement book.

"Auntie? It's Lesley."

23

"Darling! How lovely you called. And I bet I know why."

"You do?"

"Of course. You probably want to talk to me about what it's like in Israel. Hm? Isn't that it?"

"Have you been there, then?"

"You are a funny girl! I go every year, you ought to know that!"

"Well, I don't want to hear about Israel! I want to hear—" She stopped. The taboo had gone deep. She hadn't mentioned his name for three years. She pushed herself on: "I want to hear about Noah."

There was a startled silence on the other end. Then her aunt said, "Now, honey, don't put me on the spot."

"You said Daddy was wrong."

"Don't ask me to help you disobey your father, that's not fair. Your dad is your dad."

"And my brother is my brother. I need him now. Please, Auntie! We're going away for—forever." Tears suddenly came into her throat, but she pushed past them. "Help me say good-bye to him."

There was a long, thoughtful silence. Then Aunt Hannah said, "I can't do it. But you don't need me. You can find his address yourself."

"How?"

"I thought you were supposed to be smart. Your father isn't the only Shelby, N., in this town."

Of course. The telephone directory. Why hadn't she ever thought of that?

Perhaps because you don't think of outcasts having a phone.

24

T H R E E

Noah

Lesley stood outside the door of the flat where Noah lived with his Roman Catholic wife, Donna. She took a lot of deep, deep breaths.

Once, just once, she had tried to ask her father about why he had banished Noah from the family. His face had gone to marble. He had said nothing, just turned and walked away from her. That was two years ago. She'd never asked him again—never mentioned his name again, till that day in the kitchen.

But she'd asked her mother. She'd thought for sure she would tell her. Her mother was so gentle, so pliant, and she loved Lesley so much—more than ever, Lesley thought, since Noah was banished. Deep down, Lesley had some faint inkling of what her father's ban had

25

meant to her mother. . . . But only when the mention of Noah had caused Miriam Shelby to burst into tears and rush out of the room did Lesley know that there was no information to be had from her. She felt horrible, as if her mother had had an open wound and Lesley had poked a stick in it.

It was as if Noah wasn't merely disgraced, but dead.

Except that he wasn't.

He had lived for three years in the very back of her thoughts. But also here in Saskatoon. Way the other side of town from them . . . She realized now that every time she had crossed one of the bridges and gone into the downtown area, she had been looking out for him, half hoping to see him. And now she was going to. Now he was behind this door.

Noah must be twenty-two. Auntie Hannah had said he'd graduated from college and become a civil engineer. Donna was a nurse. There were no children. When Lesley had asked, "Are they happy?" Auntie Hannah had hesitated, and then said, in her honest way, "I don't know. Marriage is full enough of problems without a split on religion."

At first Lesley couldn't ring the bell—her hand just wouldn't obey her. Then she thought how angry she was with her father, how he was disrupting her life, and how he had disrupted Noah's. She thought how angry he would be with her if he knew she was here. That gave her something like a charge of electricity through her whole body. She heard the bell peal and realized she had rung it.

Steps. A man's steps. The sounds of a chain and a latch.

Then the door opened and he was there.

It was him! But changed. Now he wore dark-rimmed glasses and was taller and had filled out. But he was her sweet funny brother who had played with her and taken her places and teased her and been around till she was eleven years old. He was still the same person.

She was expecting him to drop down dead in surprise at seeing her. But one look told her Auntie Hannah had rung to warn him. So that now, instead of the absolute amazement she'd expected to see on his face, there was only a look of bemused happiness.

He reached for her and held her against him. They were both shaking—she could feel it, a deep, inner trembling. Then he held her away and stared at her and finally said shakily, "Hey, monkey face. I thought you'd never make it."

Did he mean that he'd been waiting *now,* or for years?

She couldn't stop looking at him and he couldn't stop looking at her.

"You're different," she got out at last.

"*I'm* different! Look at you! You're all growed up, kiddo. And you're even beautiful."

She couldn't say anything. She was afraid she was going to cry. She began to babble.

"Auntie spoiled the surprise, didn't she? Oh heck, never mind, are you glad to see me? I'm just so glad to see you I don't know what to say. . . ." She turned away from him to hide her brimming eyes. "This is a real cute apartment. . . . I like the pictures. . . . Where's Donna?" She had never even seen Noah's wife.

27

"She's at work. But anyway she thought we'd like to be alone."

It was a trigger. At once they both burst into an old song they'd used to croon together: "Aloooone—we wanna be—ALOOOOONE! We wanna be—toooGETHER" —deep, deep voice—"uuuh-loooooone!" They hammered it up like mad just as they used to, and suddenly a weird thing happened. Lesley's legs gave way and she slumped onto the floor, where she sat feeling too weak to do anything but laugh and then cry. And Noah sank down beside her and hugged her. He was crying a bit, too.

Later, they were in the kitchen making the cocoa they both needed. "Blood sugar," mentioned Noah. "All this emotion uses up a lot."

"So where do you keep the blood sugar?" asked Lesley, pretending to look in the cupboards.

"*Nu?* When are you off?" asked Noah suddenly. Lesley lost all desire to clown around. She turned.

"You know about it."

"Of course I know about it. Auntie Hannah keeps me posted. Putting my own selfish feelings aside, I think it's a great idea."

Lesley's jaw dropped. Everything good about this meeting felt suddenly threatened.

"Don't!" she shouted.

"Don't what?"

"Don't you side with them against me! I can't stand it if you do!"

He didn't react. He just finished making the cocoa, put

the mugs on the table in the breakfast nook, and then came and took her arm and led her firmly to the bench.

When he was sitting opposite her, he picked up his cocoa, had a sip—she was still sitting rigid with unnamable feelings—looked at her, and said, "Auntie said you were being a cowface about this. I see it's true."

Lesley muttered something between her teeth.

"What was that?"

"Damn Auntie," she said, louder.

"No fair. Without Auntie Hannah you wouldn't be here, and as a matter of fact, maybe I wouldn't either. I can't sit here and have Auntie damned, no sir. She's going to heaven if any of us are."

"Don't you dare make fun! I am so mad at you!"

"You always had a temper, fireball. Drink your cocoa and calm down."

She found herself obeying. She eyed him over the rim of the mug. Why had he this power to make her be calm? She felt her anger melting away as if the hot cocoa were pouring in over an ice cube in her stomach.

"Why wouldn't you be here without Auntie?" she asked.

"When Dad kicked me out of the family," Noah said conversationally, "I didn't take it very well. I was going on nineteen, and I'd been married a week—secretly married, as you recall, having not had the guts to tell anyone what I was up to. Donna was only just out of school, we were a pair of babes in arms. We had nowhere to live, nothing to live on. . . . Don't ask! We must have been crazy. We *were* crazy. Crazy about each other, absolutely blind to everything else. When I look back on it . . ."

"So why did you do it?"

"Get married? Oh, Les. I don't think I can explain it to you. You're growed, but you ain't that growed."

"I'm more mature than you think."

"Mature, are you? There was nothing mature about *me* at fourteen . . . or eighteen. Well. Hm. Let's see. You know about sex?"

She blushed. "Well, sure."

"And you know Catholics are very hot about *not,* before marriage?"

"Lots of people are. Dad and Mom are."

"Yeah. Well. So Donna and I had no excuses. We knew we shouldn't, but nonetheless, we did. And *after* we did, Donna felt terrible. Terribly guilty. She went to confession and the priest said, all right, you're forgiven, but don't do it again." He stopped, his chin on his fist, not looking at her. She felt an irreverent bubble of laughter coming, but she closed her throat on it firmly.

"But she did," she prompted.

"Er—*we*. Yeah. 'Fraid so."

"So then she felt terribler than ever—"

"Ten times terribler. (Surely you don't still say 'terribler'?) She said she was sure to have a baby and go to hell and goodness knows what-all, and she cried, and I felt it was my fault and that I should have kept control—" He stopped and coughed. "So we decided we'd better get hitched right away, without sort of bothering the families about it, and we thought stupidly enough that when the knot was neatly tied, all the parents would get to like the idea. I mean, we were both such lovely people, weren't we? Dumb, but lovely.

30

"The only trouble was, our religions. I went to the rabbi and he threw his hands up and said, *never,* impossible, he couldn't marry us. So I went to the priest, and he threw his hands up, too, but he said he could marry us but it would be better if I converted. Donna was mighty keen on that, too. But it took time, and meanwhile there was a baby, and hell, and everything, just around the next corner, according to Donna, so we went to the priest together.

"And he did us a deal. He'd marry us straight away, if Donna would promise that all babies would be brought up as Catholics, and if I'd promise to convert as quick as I could. And I did. And he did. And we did. And the only one who didn't was the baby, because there actually wasn't one except in Donna's conscience. What the heck are you giggling at? It wasn't funny!"

Lesley pulled herself together. She found it very difficult not to giggle when sex and babies were mentioned. "I'm sorry. It's just the way you tell it. Hey, wait. So when you told Mom and Dad that you'd converted in order to get married—"

"I actually hadn't. Not then. But I was going to, I mean I'd promised, so I was as good as. And Dad did his number. Les—have you ever seen Dad really mad? I mean, really? If you've got his temper, fireball, you'd better learn to keep hold of it good, because he scared me half to death. There was no question of talking it over, or telling him I hadn't actually converted yet. I ran out of there and I ran to Donna's—we weren't living together, of course, even though we were married, because it was a secret—and we blurted it out to *her* folks, and they had fifteen kittens between them—*shut up,* will you, I tell you it was awful!

31

We had nowhere to go. Then I thought of Auntie Hannah. She's not religious at all, she's a rationalist—"

"A what?"

"Someone who only believes what can be proved. Well. We proved to her we were married and she said, what's done is done. She settled us in her spare room and raced around to Dad and tried to talk rationally to him, but he wouldn't listen. They had a real set-to. She ended up on the Index herself."

"What's the Index?"

"The 'banned' list."

"And did you convert? Are you not a Jew anymore?"

Noah stood up and walked about the kitchen.

"Those are two entirely separate questions," he said oddly.

"What's that supposed to mean?"

"Auntie Hannah said something on that subject at the time. She said, once a Jew, always a Jew."

"But if you converted, you're a Catholic."

"Yeah. I'm a Catholic Jew."

Lesley said, *"Huh?"*

"I am two irreconcilable things at one and the same time. Which means in a way I'm a canceled-out nothing."

Lesley gave up on that one. It was too complicated, and sounded too sad.

"Why didn't Mom fight for you?" she asked. This was something that had always bothered her.

Noah heaved a sigh. "Mom is married to Dad," he said. "She'd never go against him. He comes first with her. Before either of us."

"Even if—if he's wrong? Like now?"

Noah shook his head. "He's not wrong now, Les. He's not wrong about Israel. Not for you, anyway. . . . I don't know about him and Mom."

"I don't get it. He's *doing* it for him and Mom. I think he's a—a pig-headed fanatic!"

"Where'd you get that—pig-headed fanatic?"

"I overheard Auntie Hannah. That time. She was shouting, I couldn't help it."

Noah's mouth twisted into a little smile. "Pig-headed fanatics have their points. They move the world along."

"In the wrong direction!"

"West to east. That's how the world rolls. And that's the way he's taking you. From the world of ease and plenty to the world of struggle. Just go with it, Les. This time he knows what he's doing."

"Have you even thought for one minute what I feel like?"

He sat down again, reached his hands across the table, and held hers.

"You feel very strange. Radical change always makes people feel bad, at first. But if we all just sat on our butts, in our ruts, we'd stagnate like still water. Lots of people do that. They never move, they never change, they never take a plunge, and their brains just gently decompose from lack of any real challenge."

"I don't know what you're talking about," she said fretfully. "All I know is I won't go."

"Is that so? And how are you going to get out of it?"

They stared into each other's eyes.

"You can't run away from home. You can't kill yourself. You have only two choices. To go willingly, or to go unwillingly. Which?"

"Unwillingly!" she answered instantly.

"Wrong choice. Stupid. Self-defeating. Melodramatic."

"So how would you feel?"

"At your age? Exactly like you. But it wouldn't change a thing. When something is inevitable, you had far better cooperate. That means stopping being a cowface. Start boning up on the place. Read books. I'll lend you some— I've got lots."

"Lots of books about *Israel*? Why should you?"

"Never mind, we're talking about you. Learn the language. Get your mind turned around to face it. If you don't, the adjustment when you get there is going to be tough. I mean, really tough. It's always tough for rich spoiled brats like us to live in the real world. I know what I'm talking about."

Lesley sat silent with her hands in his big warm ones. The slow tears came again and rolled down her cheeks. For the very first time she understood it was really going to happen, and it was too much to bear. There was no strength inside her to bear it with.

She put her head down on their four hands and sobbed, "Oh, Noah! I *am* a princess, just a spoiled hopeless person! I'm nothing but hot Jell-O inside. . . . Why did they give us everything? Why didn't they make us strong?"

Noah freed one hand and stroked her hair.

"That's what they're trying to do now," he said. "For you. For me it's too late. I had to do it on my own."

34

FOUR

A Peace Offering

Lesley got home from seeing Noah in a very subdued and confused state of mind.

On the bus coming back, she'd decided she wanted to change. She wanted to be what Noah wanted her to be. Sensible, cooperative, forward-looking. *Strong*. To save herself from much worse later. It made sense. Why hadn't it made sense when her parents had urged her to be that way?

Maybe because she loved Noah and she couldn't feel she loved them.

Noah, when he took her to the bus, had said, "Nobody's all of a piece. There's no such thing as an all-black hat." She knew about black hats and white hats from her dad, who read a lot of thrillers for relaxation. It meant baddies and goodies. But Noah was saying there was no such thing, not completely—that baddies (like her father!) could have a good side. Like being kind most of the time. And clever.

He showed he could be both, that very evening.

When, having crept upstairs as usual without speaking to anyone, she opened the door to her bedroom, she found two dress boxes on the bed: one big, and one still bigger.

These boxes, with "Shelby's" on them in sloping black writing, were well known to her. Her father usually brought them home around special occasions like birthdays.

She stood looking at the boxes. She knew what they were full of—new clothes for her to try on and choose from. And as she took the top off the smaller box and heard the luscious rustle of tissue paper, she understood something else.

This was her father's peace offering.

Inside the first box was a gorgeous dress. Breathstopped, she lifted it out and held it against herself. It wasn't strapless. It wasn't anything like she'd have chosen herself. The top was purply blue velvet, sleeveless, very simple, with a scooped neck and a wide matching satin bow across the waist. The waist was loose-fitting, almost straight up and down. Below the bow, the material changed to tiny white lace ruffles that went all the way down to the hem.

And it was *short*. Well above the knee—the very latest in minidresses. It was *next* year's model, probably not even in the store yet—it just screamed "1967," even though it was still only 1966!

36

In the same box were two pairs of patterned white pantyhose with just a hint of glitter, and adorable blue suede pumps with a tiny heel.

Lesley forgot everything. Her anger, her rebellion, the future—everything except the dance and how she would look at it, with her hair in a sleek black pageboy like Jackie Kennedy's, and everyone wearing *old-fashioned* long formals except her!

Clutching the dress, she rushed out of the room and down the wide staircase. Her father was just coming out of his study. She flung herself on him, dress and all.

"Daddy! It's just gorgeous! It's the swooshiest dress *ever!*"

He put his arms around her for a moment and gave her a very tight hug. "I ordered it from New York. . . ." Then he let her go, and said, "What about the rest?"

"What rest? Oh . . . I didn't open the other box yet! Is it winter clothes? Not—it's not cashmere sweaters, is it?" she asked, alight with excitement.

"Go have a peek."

She raced upstairs again. Laying the dress reverently across her chair, she lifted the top off the larger box.

There were no cashmere sweaters. These were hot-weather clothes. A yellow linen pants suit with bell-bottoms, two one-piece bathing suits, sundresses, fashion tops, shorts . . .

As she looked through them, all her happiness suddenly died. She slumped down on the edge of the bed amid the rustling paper and the lids and the bright, costly clothes.

These were for Israel.

She felt herself getting angry again. Her father had tricked her! She couldn't go on "sulking" after throwing herself around his neck and thanking him like that for the dress. How she wished she'd opened the bigger box first! Then she'd have seen what he was up to!

She didn't know what to do now. She temporized by trying the new things on. They were all terrific. Her father knew her size, and her tastes. She paraded before her floor-length mirror in the yellow pants suit, feeling the flares stroking her ankles as she moved. . . .

Perhaps if she could go in all-new clothes, looking really swooshy, much better dressed than any of the Israeli girls obviously, perhaps . . . it wouldn't be so bad, being there.

For the first time, she tried to imagine what it might be like. Till now, all she'd imagined was leaving home.

She fingered one of the bright swimsuits. It would be hot there. Israel was right on the Mediterranean. . . . Having lived all her life on the prairie, and seen the sea only once, on a trip to Vancouver, she thought living near it might be . . . well, exciting. Not worth leaving her river for, but—well, you couldn't swim in the river.

What would the other kids be like? Would there be formal dances and volleyball and basketball and dating? Since the scene in Lee's hall, when he'd let her down, she hadn't felt so keen on him (though she was still going with him to the dance). Maybe it wasn't wholly disloyal to be thinking about, well, about Israeli boys.

They must be pretty tough. They all had to go into the army at eighteen. So did the girls! Lee'd been right—she'd checked. Of course, eighteen was years off, but—it sure would give her something to write to Sonia about—being a soldier!

And what would school be like there? And what sort of place would they live in?

Well, one thing. They'd still be rich. The store had sold for thousands and thousands of dollars, they could buy any house they liked, with a big garden. . . . Maybe they could have their own pool! Sure, why not? And she could give pool parties, and invite her own gang, when she had a gang, and have a band, and barbecues, and . . .

"Lesley, come down to supper, bubbalink, okay?"

Her mother hadn't called her "bubbalink" since all the horror started. Her father must have told her the row was all over. Was it?

She looked around swiftly. There it was: the plastic shopping bag Noah had given her, full of books. Books about Israel. She tipped them onto the carpet and spread them out like playing cards.

Novels. History-of-Israel books. Even a teach-yourself-Hebrew. She picked that one up and turned it over. Very well thumbed. Noah must have bought it secondhand. It couldn't be that he'd been using it himself—why should he want to teach himself Hebrew?

Lesley looked inside the book. All those strange letter shapes . . . nothing familiar, nothing to get a grip on . . . they even wrote from right to left. Could Noah have tackled that? When he wasn't even a Jew anymore?

Once a Jew, always a Jew.

"Les! C'mon down, it's getting cold!"

Hurriedly she scooped all the books back into the bag

39

and hid it in the back of her big wardrobe. The war might be over, but she wasn't going to offer unconditional surrender. Any boning up she did would be done in absolute secrecy. It was still a terrible, terrible thing her father was doing to her. She was not about to give even a polka-dotted black-hat like him any satisfaction. Not even if the dress had come from *Paris*.

Arrival

"Look, Lesley! Israel!"

Lesley, sitting next to the plane window, glanced from her magazine out and downward past the huge silver wing. Below stretched a jigsaw country of dark cream and green, dotted with clusters of tiny white boxes that were buildings. Most of the vast pattern she could see was the misty blue ocean.

"It looks very small."

"It *is* small," said her father, sounding both reverent and thrilled. "Small and great."

Lesley went back to her magazine. She was not going to let him see the surge of excitement that had gone through her, looking down and seeing her new world spread out below.

41

Five weeks had passed since her first meeting with Noah. Since then she had played things cool. She had not sulked again after the night of the blue-and-white dress (later worn with sensational success at her last Canadian school dance), but she had stayed aloof, refusing to bestow open interest on the family adventure. But she wasn't rude and she wasn't mutinous. She cultivated an air of quiet, *mature* resignation. She thought she'd pulled it off pretty well.

Her parents seemed relieved—and gratifyingly puzzled. Little did they know about her secret sessions behind the locked door of her room with Noah's books.

She had read a lot about Israel now. Novels like *Exodus, New Face in the Mirror, Dust, An End to Running.* And nonfiction, too, books about the early immigrants from Russia, the time when Israel was still Palestine and the British ruled it and eventually had to leave because of all the violence between Arabs and Jews. About when the displaced Jews of Europe were flocking to Israel and being turned away (but getting in just the same), and about the War of Independence in 1948 against all the Arab countries around Israel, which Israel won, and about the years since, years of tension and trial when nobody expected the State to survive, let alone prosper—but somehow it did.

And about the Holocaust. The horror which, it seemed to Lesley, made it absolutely necessary that the Jews should have a country of their own, to run to in time of trouble, and from which to defend themselves.

She couldn't remain indifferent or hostile anymore after she began to understand. She even began to feel that, after all, Canada was not their country, because in Canada there were people like Sonia who didn't even know where Israel was, who were quite ignorant of what the Jews had suffered.

She cried a lot when the time to leave came, just the same. But it wasn't the furious, desperate, rebellious crying she had done at first. It was pure sadness. And it was not about leaving Lee, despite his having kissed her after the dance and promised to write to her. It was mostly for leaving Noah, whom she'd found only to lose again.

She had given all his books back to him at their last meeting. She admitted they'd changed her. And they'd both been so sad. . . . But he had braced her up with his grown-up strength, and given her a private, secret letter to carry with her, to read and to keep, and they had promised undying brother- and sisterhood, and contacts whenever they were possible without their parents knowing.

And now they were landing. Lesley kept talking to Noah in her head. *We're here, Noah, we're here! Oh, I wish you were here with us!*

"Come on, bubbalink, you bring the coats and don't forget your flight bag! Oh, leave that silly magazine, you don't want that!" Lesley laid the *Maclean's* on the seats among all the leftovers from the flight.

Bureaucracy laid hold of them like some big machine. They were "processed" with other new immigrants, and placed for the time being in a big ugly block in Tel Aviv called an Absorption Center.

Lesley, who thought she had prepared herself, found she hadn't. Not at all. Her aloofness had prevented her asking enough sensible questions. . . . She had expected them to live in a luxury hotel until her parents had bought a house and got them settled. She got a very nasty shock at the smallness of their apartment in the center—apartment! It was two small, well-used rooms with plain walls, tiled floors, and a few bits of gimcrack furniture.

She had to sleep on a hard modern sofa in the living room. She had nowhere to hang her clothes, and they lived out of their suitcases. There was no kitchen. They ate in a big, noisy, serve-yourself cafeteria with some sixty other families. Meals were awful. There was nothing she was used to. Fancy eating cream cheese and salad for breakfast! And horrible goulash and lumpy stewed chicken innards for lunch!

She hated this place. There was no privacy. The walls were thin and there were always, always other people. And a lot of those at the center weren't—well, they looked poor and they weren't very well mannered, or even, Lesley thought, very clean.

"Don't look down on them," warned her father sharply when he saw her lip curl at a fat, dark-skinned woman with a loud voice and a lot of children. "They're Jews like us." Lesley said nothing, but what she thought was "They may be Jews, but they're not like us."

Her newfound "cool" wavered and crashed.

"Why do we have to be in this ghastly place?" she'd wailed on the first evening, when she was still in shock.

"Nearly all new immigrants start in a center," her

44

mother explained, "while they make arrangements to settle. And we have to learn Hebrew."

"But I know—" Lesley began. Her mother turned quickly. "I know I shouldn't fuss," Lesley said feebly. She had made a good start on Hebrew with the help of Noah's teach-yourself book; at least, she thought she had. She knew the letters and a few simple words and sentences. It had been very hard to learn anything, and in fact it turned out, on the first day of lessons, that she'd hardly begun.

A brisk young woman teacher marched into the beginners' class—consisting of twenty people from the ages of fourteen to sixty—and began to teach. *In Hebrew*. There was a rustle of dismay. The teacher blithely ignored it. Hardly any of the students could understand a word. Lesley couldn't believe what was happening.

"Why doesn't she teach us in English?" she asked afterward indignantly.

"Because there are people here from several countries," explained her mother. "Besides, according to the latest ideas, foreign languages are taught by the Natural Method—the way you learned your own, by listening."

Lesley thought this was out-and-out garbage. If you couldn't understand anything, how could you possibly learn? She wished she'd kept the teach-yourself book. She could do a million times better on her own.

The regime was like a boarding school for all ages. For six hours a day, six days a week, everyone above the age of fourteen was expected to study. Only the heads of family were excused when they had to go out to visit various offices to do with settlement.

Her father came back from the office round in a state of frustration that he couldn't always hide, even though he was determined to see only the best in Israel.

"The lines," he muttered. "The endless lines! And when you reach the window, they send you off to another line somewhere else!"

Lesley's mother did attend every lesson. For Lesley there was something unreal about seeing her mother bent over their cheap little table in the evenings, wrestling with homework.

For herself, she was so irritated by not being able at once to grasp *something* that she felt rebellion taking her over again. After the first week, she decided to quit.

Her mother (who was not in her class) came back from lessons at lunchtime next day and said, "Where have you been all morning? Your teacher asked about you and I didn't know what to say."

"I'm not going anymore."

Her mother narrowed her eyes. "Lesley, don't start this. Don't, I'm warning you. We all have to learn. Do you think it's easy for me?"

Lesley shrugged sharply. "I don't know."

"Well, let me tell you it isn't. It's much harder for all of us older people, sitting down to study for the first time in years and being scolded like kids when we can't learn quickly enough. Do you think that's fun?"

"You chose it," Lesley said shortly. "I didn't."

Her mother began to speak, then closed her mouth. She slammed out of the apartment on her way to the cafeteria without asking Lesley if she wanted to come with her. Lesley had never seen her mother act that way—so tense and upset.

She decided not to have lunch with the "hungry hundreds." She left the center and went for a walk to help her think.

Everyone said Tel Aviv was an ugly town, but Lesley rather liked it. She liked the apartment blocks, some of them on stilts, with balconies all done up like rooms, with furniture and pictures on the walls. People came out on them and sat and read the papers and listened to the radio and played cards and ate their meals and watched the world go by. Lesley felt as if the people who lived there were sharing their lives with her.

And she liked the sidewalk cafés where, even though it was December, you could sit in the sunshine and have something that reminded you of home—real coffee (not the tasteless muck at the center) or a Coke, or a hot dog. You could buy an English-language newspaper and read the American baseball scores, or listen to American pop from the radios everyone seemed to carry around, and pretend you were on vacation and that when it ended, you could go right home.

That's what she did. And when she'd eaten her (kosher) hot dog she unzipped a pocket of her shoulder bag and took out Noah's letter.

She'd already read it several times, and knew parts of it by heart, but whenever she was feeling low, she read it again.

Hi, sis,

The more I think about how I want this letter to be, the more difficult it gets. What I don't *want it to be is an exercise in brotherly preaching. I know I want you to get back* on good terms with the family, but who am I to talk about that? I fouled up pretty good in that department. But they still love you, and what they're doing now is tied up with that. You won't believe it for a while yet, but it's true.

Perhaps now you've read up a bit, you can see their viewpoint better. Now you know the background. The thing is, Dad and Mom are Jews, children of Jews who were children of Jews all the way back four thousand years. The Jews have had a bad time, living in other people's countries. Yes, I know, Canada has been good to us, we've been tolerated—give or take the odd bit of anti-Semitism that pops up now and then when you least expect it. Nobody's ever said anything to you about being Jewish? You're lucky. They will, sooner or later. You can bet Dad's heard plenty of cracks, going up the ladder. Maybe somebody who was envious of him finally made one crack too many. Maybe he's gotten tired of feeling he has to run harder than everyone else in order to stay in the same place. Who knows. That's the way things are, and always have been. Not everyone can get used to it.

Dad's decided to tear his Canadian roots up and put them down again in the only place in the world where he can be a fully integrated Jew, and where you can grow up that way, not a Canadian not knowing what being Jewish really means, if anything. Dad's right, you can't half be a Jew. I'm trying to do it, every day, and I'm here to tell you it doesn't work. Only you and Auntie Hannah know this. Donna doesn't, and I don't want her to because she might think I was sorry I married her. I'm not. I love her. I just wish she was Jewish. There. Now it's out.

Now, what I want to warn you about is this. Dad's

doing this for himself as well as for you. I think it's right—for you. I'm not so sure it's right for him. He's fifty. That's old to start afresh. I just hope he won't go to extremes, but as we both know, he's an extremes-going sort of guy. What he should do is have the same life-style there as here. I know that's what you're expecting. Don't hold your breath. Knowing him, I'd look out for some surprises.

As to Mom, I'm frankly worried. That's why I want you to be close to them, to love them through this. They'll need you. You think you're the poor victim, but if you're sensible and put your back into adjusting, you're going to sail through it, compared to them. I think it's going to be tougher on them than they have any idea of. How I wish I were going to be there to cushion them a bit! But as I can't, kiddo, you'll have to do it on your own.

A bit of a tall order for a little 'un. But you'll grow.

As for you, all you need to remember is that princesses ain't popular outside of palaces. And there aren't many of those about in Israel. There's an old saying that people are the same everywhere. Take it from me, they're not. Israel is not Canada. Israelis are not Canadians. Israelis have never known what it is to feel really safe, for one thing. That makes people tough and it makes them nervous. You've got to allow for that.

If you don't write to me and keep me posted, I'm going to come out there and throw you in the ocean, head first. I'll write back when you can find a way so Dad doesn't get wind of it.

Love, and I mean it,
Noah

49

As always, the letter made her feel better. She folded it up and went back to the center, saying in her head, "Oh, *o-kay, o-kay,* you win!" She would give her mother a hug and tell her she'd go to lessons tomorrow.

But then, as she was going through the hallway at the center, she bumped into a girl in her class named Diana.

Diana was English and Lesley couldn't stand her—talk about a princess, they have them in England, too, and there it means "snob." She turned up her nose at everybody. So Lesley was surprised when she stopped with a seemingly friendly smile and said, "I hear you're leaving soon."

Lesley said, "What?"

"Oh," said Diana, all innocent, "didn't your parents tell you? Your mother told my mother that your father's fixed you up in a kibbutz."

Lesley didn't reply. She couldn't. She just stared at Diana dumbly.

"Mummy was quite surprised. She said yours was the last family she could imagine in a kibbutz. You're all such *city* kind of people. You'll have to put all your posh clothes away. They just wear old *schmattes* in kibbutz, and how will you like the farm work? All those smelly animals . . . Rather you than me, I must say!"

And off she went with a toss of her head.

Lesley felt all the old rage come flooding back on her like a tidal wave. She rushed straight up to the apartment and threw the door open.

Her parents were sitting on the sofa. They turned as she burst in.

"What's this I hear!" she cried accusingly. "We're going to a stinking kibbutz, and you never even told me!"

50

They both jumped up, and her father said guiltily, "We were going to tell you tonight, Les!" He threw her mother a look, and her mother turned red. "Couldn't you have kept quiet till we'd told her? This place is a hotbed of gossip, you know that!"

"I'm sorry—I never thought—"

"It's true, then!" cried Lesley in dismay.

"Yes, it's true. Sit down and let's talk about it. We'll tell you what a kibbutz is like."

"I *know* what they're like! I've read about them!" she shouted, giving the game away. They looked at each other in surprise. "They're communal farms, where nobody owns anything, or makes any money, or has anything everybody else doesn't have, and they live in little tiny rooms, and do farm work, and they take the kids away from their parents!" All her resolutions were broken, she was crying like a baby, her nose was running, and she felt as bad as she had in the very beginning.

"Lesley—"

"You won't be satisfied till you've broken up the whole family!" she sobbed. "Going to extremes! You're always going to extremes!" Her father's jaw dropped, whether from anger or astonishment she couldn't tell, and she didn't care. "Why, why, *why* are we going *there*? Why can't we keep our—our life-style, why can't we live like rich people? We are rich, we're *rich,* and there are rich people here, and nice houses, I've seen them—we don't have to be dirty peasants just because we've come to this stupid country!"

She rushed through into the bedroom and threw herself down on her parents' hard bed and thrashed her wet face back and forth on the cotton bedcover till she'd made a dent smeared with tears and nose slime. She kicked her legs and thrashed her arms and howled aloud. When her mother came after her, she threw her hands off.

"Get away from me! I hate you both, I hate you, you're selfish, you're stupid, leave me alone!"

Her mother left her.

After a long, long time she pulled herself together, crawled upright, and washed her face in the basin. She felt terrible. She'd behaved like ten princesses, all of them babies. She'd let Noah down. But it didn't alter how she felt.

She went through into the little living room. Her parents were in there, talking. They stopped as she came in. For a moment she stood there, thinking viciously: *I'll punish them. I'll tell them I've been to see Noah. That'll pay them out.* But she couldn't do it. And there was nowhere to go in this beastly little place, nowhere to shut yourself in and be alone. It occurred to her that the kibbutz would be like this. Just like this. How could she bear it?

"I want to go to bed," she said sullenly.

Her parents stood up at once. They both looked very upset.

"I'll help you make your bed up," said her mother.

"Just leave me alone," said Lesley.

She didn't sleep for hours. She imagined the kibbutz—a place of drab barracks in the midst of a dreary treeless wilderness, full of robot-like figures all dressed alike in grayish uniform. She forgot she hated her parents, and imagined being torn from her mother's arms and dragged away screaming by some vaguely Russian-looking peasants

52

with brutal faces and guns. Her mental scenario was so real to her it made her cry again. Her whole life was ruined. She even felt she hated Noah for telling her such lies, like that she would be all right, that she'd adjust, that she wasn't a victim.

I am a victim, she thought. *I'll never adjust to this place. Never.* She lay there swamped in pity for herself till at last she fell asleep.

S I X

Kibbutz

The kibbutz truck bumped around the final bend in the road.

They'd been driving for nearly two hours. Tel Aviv and the center were miles behind them. They'd crossed a wide plain, been through a dusty little town, and for the past ten minutes had been going downhill. The air had been getting steadily warmer. It felt as if they were entering a tropical country. They'd passed a lot of bright green broad-leaved tree-like plants that the driver said were bananas, and others that he told them were mangoes. Up ahead, Lesley, through the truck wind-screen, could see what appeared to be a forest of palm trees.

"We are arrived," said the driver. "Here is Kibbutz Kfar Orde."

They drew up in a large unpaved parking area, and the Shelbys climbed out and looked around.

Lesley could see at once that it was nothing like she'd imagined. The buildings were far from barrack-like. They were white, with red roofs and painted shutters. And the place was not drab and treeless. There were trees and gardens everywhere. Very beautiful, exotic gardens, quite different from at home.

A thin, middle-aged woman came to greet them. The only gray thing about her was her hair—she was dressed in casual but quite colorful clothes. She looked rather severe, but friendly, too.

"I am Ayala, from the absorption committee," she said, shaking hands with them. She looked straight into Lesley's eyes and said, "Shalom, Leslee. *Baruch ha'ba'a.* That means 'welcome.' "

"I know," said Lesley.

Ayala led them along narrow, concrete paths, through park-like gardens and past some large one-story buildings.

"That is our very new dining hall. That is our social club."

"Where do you keep the farm?" asked Lesley's father cheerfully.

"Ah, we hide that!" said Ayala. "All the working part is over there behind those trees."

"I can smell the cows."

"The smell we cannot hide," she said, and Nat Shelby laughed.

55

"I like it, I like it!" He seemed in very good spirits now they were here. But Lesley noticed her mother was quiet.

Now they were walking along beside a tall chain-link fence. Beyond was a road, and some distance beyond that was a sort of cut in the earth like a ravine.

"What's down there?" Lesley asked.

"The river," said Ayala.

"Oh! There's a river here!"

Ayala, who was walking ahead, turned and gave her a funny look. "You didn't look it up on a map?" she said, only she said "mep." "That's the river Jordan. Here we are."

She led the parents up some steps into one of the long, white buildings, but Lesley had stopped dead under the pepper trees. The river Jordan . . . That couldn't be *the* Jordan, like in the spirituals? *"Deep river, my home is on the Jordan. . . ."* A strange prickle of excitement crept up Lesley's spine. It was like finding out that a legend was true and alive.

She followed the others. Inside the front door, which had a fly-screen window in it, was a very small porch containing a simple table, two chairs, a sink in a cupboard, and a little fridge like an orange box. Beyond that, through another door, a living room, very simply furnished, and leading off that a bedroom, just big enough to hold a double bed and some built-in cupboards. When Lesley looked around for the rest of the apartment, she suddenly realized this was it. There was no more.

Her father was running his fingers happily along the bookshelves that occupied almost the whole of one wall.

"The man who used to live here was a teacher," said Ayala. "If you like, we'll take some of the shelves down."

"I threw out all the escape garbage I used to read," he said. "I'll have time to read some real books now."

"If we don't work you too hard!" said Ayala with a smile.

Nat Shelby laughed heartily.

Lesley said rather shrilly, "And where do I sleep?"

"With the others of your age," said Ayala. "They're expecting you. When your parents have asked their questions, we will go there."

Lesley looked at her mother. She was staring around with a blank look, and Lesley guessed at her feelings. She'd accepted the shortcomings of the center—that was temporary. But this . . . this was to be her home! No proper kitchen, no proper bathroom, only a shower, no space, no nice things . . . She opened her mouth as if she had a question, but nothing came out.

Lesley's father put his arm around her and said in a firm, happy voice, "We have no more to ask at the moment, thank you. This is all just great." He touched some things that had been left on the table: a bowl of fruit, a copper vase of flowers, a chocolate cake with some Hebrew lettering on it in white frosting. "Swell idea—a special welcome. We appreciate it."

"It's our custom for newcomers," said Ayala briskly. "Are you ready, Leslee?"

Tears sprang to her mother's eyes. "When will we see you again, baby?" she said in a wobbly voice.

Lesley felt a sudden wave of embarrassment and quickly

said, "Oh, Mom, for gosh sakes, I'll be right back. Come on, er—Ila, let's go!"

And she escaped. Later she was to think ruefully, *So much for the nightmare Russian peasants.* Nothing but her mother's tears had been needed to propel her off into her separate life.

As they walked along the paths, Lesley said, "Is that really the Jordan? *The* Jordan, I mean?"

"Yes, of course. Here the river is the border."

Lesley frowned, wishing she'd found out a bit more. Her father had mentioned that the kibbutz was "on the border," but she wasn't clear what it meant.

"What border?"

Ayala gave her that funny look again. It made Lesley feel small.

"The border with Jordan. That's Jordan, beyond the river." She pointed to some rounded, pinkish, scrub-dotted hills on the distant horizon. "Enemy territory."

"Oh." She cleared her throat. She didn't want Ayala to think she was afraid, because she wasn't, just curious. "Is there ever any shooting?"

"Well, you see the army patrols, but it's quiet enough. They're farmers over there, like us."

"Can you see them?"

"Of course. Tilling their fields. We could call across to each other, if only we weren't enemies."

This was very interesting. But before Lesley could ask any more questions, they arrived at a big, square, beat-up–looking building.

"This is it."

Lesley stopped. *"This?"*

"Not quite what you've been used to, perhaps?" said Ayala dryly.

"No," said Lesley feelingly. The interest, excitement even, evaporated, leaving a hollow in her stomach that she tried to fight with a deep sigh. Then she swallowed. From inside came loud, strident voices—Hebrew voices. The nearness of the enemy hadn't frightened her as those voices did.

"Daddy said—" she croaked out, and cleared her throat again.

"Nu?"

"He told me people in this kibbutz came from England mostly."

"Not me, but some do. So?"

"So they speak English, right?"

"Ah," Ayala said, and laughed a little. "But you were not thinking their *children* are speaking English, so you would not have to learn *Ivrit?*"

Lesley swallowed again, and nodded.

"I am sorry, Leslee," said Ayala quite kindly. Then she asked, "You want I should come in with you, to introduce to you your group?"

The sympathy in her voice brought out a perverse defiance in Lesley. She suddenly made up her mind to show no weakness. Standing there with one foot on the steps leading into her new life, she made a lightning but compelling promise to herself.

She was scared, but she wouldn't show it. If these Israeli kids were mean to her, she would be mean right back—

meaner. If she was lonely, she would hide it. If as miserable as she fully expected to be—well, she would hide that, too. And she would never, never cry, not where anyone could see her.

"No, thank you," she answered Ayala. "I'll go in alone."

She braced herself like a soldier going into battle and marched up the steps.

She found herself in a long corridor with doors along it, mostly open, and it was from there that the voices came. They must be bedrooms. Below the long window on the other side of the corridor were benches, littered with people's belongings. Some pictures and creeping plants hung between the doors. The tiled floor had recently been wiped, and there were bare footprints all over it.

Standing in a group at the end of this corridor were two girls and a boy. They wore faded jeans and T-shirts. One of the girls was plump and had frizzy red hair. The other was slender and very pretty. Her hair was long, straight, and blond. Neither wore any makeup. The boy was just a boy, very tanned.

The pretty one saw her first. She nudged the others and then called, *"Shalom!"*

Lesley's mouth was too dry to answer, but she stood still while they came toward her. Suddenly something very curious happened. Her smart yellow pants suit began to prickle, and the brooch on her collar, which had a big mock topaz in it, grew so heavy that she reached up to touch it. Her hair—carefully arranged and lacquered in her best Jackie Kennedy style for this challenging occasion—

burned her head, and her lips felt greasy under their lip-stick. The very worst thing was the silly little yellow bow on her head, just where the bulge of back-combed hair began. Unable to help herself, she snatched it off.

The three had reached her now. Though they looked her in the face, she felt they were all, even the boy, taking in every detail of her appearance and finding her ludicrously gussied up. She wanted the tiles to open up under her.

They were all asking her questions.

"I don't speak Hebrew," she said with as much dignity as possible.

They exchanged puzzled looks.

"You must to learn," said the boy slowly.

"Don't you learn English?"

"No so good," he said. "Our teacher not know how to teach good."

"But your parents are English!"

"So what? Parents is not teachers!"

"You want to see room for sleep?" asked the frizzy one.

Lesley allowed herself to be led into one of the rooms. It was a small square bedroom with four beds in it. Four beds? Was it possible that she was not to have a room of her own? They were all tidily made under striped cotton coverlets, except one, which had heaps of clothes and bits and pieces all over it. In that corner there were posters on the wall, including one of the Beatles, and Lesley was puzzled to see several model airplanes dangling from the ceiling. Each bed had a shabby rug beside it and a shelf over it. One shelf was empty.

"This bed your," said the fat, frizzy girl. "You put books

here." She pointed to the shelf. "This the bed of me." She pointed to the one opposite.

"I sleeping here," said the pretty one, indicating one of the other beds.

"And this my," said the boy, and plumped down among the heap of rubbish on the fourth bed.

Lesley's mouth actually fell open and for several seconds she couldn't utter a word. Her face must have been comical, because all three burst out laughing.

"But I can't sleep in a room with a *boy*!" Lesley almost shouted.

They kept laughing and nodded their heads like dummies. With gestures and a few words, they tried to tell her it was okay, she would get used to it. She turned her face away, her vow all but broken already as tears of helplessness came into her eyes against her will. But as they noticed, and stopped laughing, she stiffened herself and asked, "Where do I keep my clothes?"

"What?"

"My clothes!" She plucked at her suit, frustration rampaging inside her. The pretty girl said, "Ah, *begadim!*" and opened a small, old-fashioned wardrobe. It looked almost full, but there was one shelf vacant, and by pushing all the loaded hangers to one end, the girl exposed a short length of rail.

"That for you," she said.

Incredible. After what she'd had at home?

"It's too small! I have three suitcases full of stuff!"

The fat girl pointed to the pants suit. "Very nice, but like this you not need." Then, with much giggling and consulting the other two for words, she explained with her strong accent, "Summair—short trousair, shirt, *beged-yam*—for swim." She gave a demonstration of breaststroke. "Wintair—long trousair, sweatair, hot coat hang outside. One-two dress or trousair for Shabbat." (Lesley knew this was for Saturday, the Jewish Sabbath.) "They stay in other place. Also, *begadim* for work. Here, only thing for school and go home to parents. This enough place."

The others rewarded this lengthy speech with loud applause. The boy then pointed to himself and rattled off triumphantly, "My name is Ofer what is your name?" This was clearly a gambit they had had to learn by heart in their unsuccessful English lessons.

"Lesley."

"My name is Shula," said the fat one.

"My name is Aviva," said the pretty one. "You want see other?"

Lesley wanted nothing less at the moment. She felt overwhelmed and wanted only to be left alone. But Ofer was already out of the room, and she heard his strident voice calling along the corridor. Shouts answered him, and suddenly the little room was crowded with strange faces and she was drowning in impossible names. Only a few, like Esther, Ruth, and David (pronounced Davveed), she even recognized. The others were just noises.

Lesley knew with her mind that they were trying to make her welcome, but the more they tried, the more alien she felt. The more she eyed their clothes, the more she longed to dive under the bed to hide her own. The more she thought of living—actually living, day after day and

63

night after night—in this little box, with no space, no privacy, no room to breathe her own breath or silence to think her own thoughts, the more sure she became that Noah and her father were crazy, and that she herself would shortly be crazy, too.

S E V E N

A Transformation

She was dismayed to find that her one wish now was to flee back to her parents. But she set her teeth, and allowed the crowd of kids to shepherd her about the building that she must now call home.

She was astonished to find that they lived and studied all in the same building—at the end of the corridor was a roomy but unsmart classroom, with chipped greenish blackboards and double desks intricately carved with Hebrew initials.

"This desk of me. You want to sit next?" asked Shula.

Lesley would rather have had Aviva, the pretty one, as a desk partner, but Aviva hadn't asked her.

"Oh, okay," she said, hoping Shula didn't sweat. At home what you looked like had a great deal to do with how popular you were. She didn't want to be the friend of someone who had no other friends.

She was shown the shower rooms (at least there the boys and girls were separated!) and the hook on which she would hang her towel and washbag.

Outside was a spiky lawn, badly worn in places (were those posts for a volleyball net?) and a fishpond they had made themselves. Next they took her to the "children's farm." Lesley liked animals, in theory—her family had never kept a pet because the house was too beautiful to risk spoiling it, but she'd always wanted one—but this was not cute dogs and cats, but pens of sheep, goats, poultry, some monkeys, and several beautiful but noisy peacocks. There were children around, taking care of them.

"You like to work with animal?"

"I don't know."

"What work you like?"

"You mean, schoolwork? I like math, and—"

"No, no. Work-work. After lesson, we work two hour. Where you want to work? Kitchen? Chicken? Field?"

Chicken? *Field?* Lesley shook her head. "I don't know," she said again, feeling absolutely feeble and terribly apprehensive. Diana had been right about dirty farm work!

After that, she was borne off to the center of the kibbutz to inspect the communal dining hall.

The children clearly found this big modern building a source of great pride. It was the newest thing in the kibbutz, and, Lesley thought, quite the ugliest. The scores of tables, arranged in rows, were covered with Formica; the chairs were plain wood; the walls bare except for a weird mural made of what looked like the floor scrapings of a machine shop. There was a long hatch through which meals were served, and—a great novelty, this, apparently—a tap which gave iced soda-water. There wasn't a bit of color except the curtains, which were a sort of orange. Of course, beyond the windows were views of the gardens and the far-off pink hills.

"Beautiful, not?" Aviva asked her, evidently eager for her praise.

"Mm," said Lesley. "A bit bare."

"A bit bare" more or less described Lesley's feelings about the kibbutz altogether. Bare of decoration, bare of elegance, bare of comfort. After the luxuries of home, it was hard not to look down on such plainness.

As they returned to the *kitta,* as the others called the classroom-house, Lesley saw Ofer and two other boys come staggering across the lawn with her three heavy suitcases.

"This your 'stuff'?" asked Shula.

Having looked forward to unpacking all her luscious new clothes before an admiring audience, Lesley now felt she'd rather die. Every garment in those cases shouted "princess!" They would hate her.

"Under the bed," said Lesley to the boys. "I'll unpack later."

"Now! Now!" chorused the girls. "We want to see!"

"No." Frantically she sought a distraction. "Now you teach me Hebrew—*Ivrit.*"

They broke into a whoop of approval and began rushing about pointing at objects and naming them in the words she had begun to learn at the center. She imitated them easily enough, but keeping them in her head was another matter. "What if I never learn!" she thought in sudden terror. "Oh, Noah!"

The crowd of kids now began to drift away. It was 4 P.M., time for "four o'clock meal."

"You go to your parents now?" Shula asked. "You know to find?"

"Soon," said Lesley. Shula nodded.

"Lahitra'ot!"

" 'Bye."

She was alone. She knew she should go now, but she was afraid to face her mother's tearfulness, afraid of how unwilling she would be, later, to come back. So she stayed in the big empty building.

First she sat and did nothing but stare out of the window. It had a screen on it, which was torn at one corner, allowing a few mosquitoes in. One shutter was broken and flapped noisily in the afternoon wind.

The curtains, like her bedcover, were faded and limp. She thought of the crisp bright fabrics in her bedroom at home that she'd chosen herself, the wallpaper and glossy paint that were renewed every two years before it could ever get shabby. . . . Shelves for her books, a deep-pile cream carpet, a battery of closets, luxury armchair, padded bed head, her own shining bathroom with turquoise fittings . . .

Tears were coming. She got up quickly. It wouldn't be

68

breaking her vow to cry now, but she thought it would be good practice if she could control it.

She pulled out a suitcase and opened it. For a moment she looked at the neatly tissued layers of lovely things she'd been saving. Then she closed it again, and opened the one she'd been living out of for the past weeks.

She burrowed in it, pulled out a few bits of underwear, two towels, her washing things, and her old stuff—her jeans and knock-about shoes and sloppy sweaters. She hadn't wanted to bring these, but her mother had packed them anyhow. She chose two of her simplest dresses for Shabbat. From the third suitcase she took some books and her most precious possession: her secret box.

This had been made for her by Noah in his carpentry class when he was fifteen and she was almost eight. It was beautiful, with an inlaid pattern on the lid, and it locked with a little padlock. She kept the key around her neck in a big locket. Noah's letter, some school photos, little mementos she'd had from childhood, and her journal were kept here, safely locked up.

She'd noticed the others wore no jewelry other than an occasional Star of David on a fine chain. The locket, like her topaz brooch, looked show-offy, much too big. She took it off and looked for a hiding place. In her bedroom at home there were dozens; here you had to use your ingenuity.

At last she discovered that the mattresses were made of a kind of foam rubber that had little square pockets in it. Making a tiny cut in the mattress cover with her nail scissors, she dropped the locket, with the key inside it, into

69

the pocket. The box she put on the shelf. She thought of stowing it under the bed, but figured if she hid it, it would only make the others more curious.

The box took up most of the shelf, but she found room for a few of her favorite books. Here she couldn't resist choosing her most "intellectual" ones for display. Silly, really, because the kids wouldn't be able to read the titles, but they enabled her to hang on to the feeling of superiority that had been oozing away all day.

Now she took her washbag and towel into the shower room and shut the door. She took a shower (the first of how many?) and scrubbed all traces of lipstick off, and washed the curl out of her hair. She combed it straight and put on her old *schmattedic* clothes and then looked at herself critically in the mirror.

A new Lesley confronted her—a Lesley you couldn't tell from an Israeli girl. In Canada she would be ashamed to go out looking so—so plain. Yet the fancy clothes, the fancy hair, the makeup, the jewelry—they'd *burned* her. She couldn't have gone on wearing them. Not here.

She remembered the novel she'd read, *New Face in the Mirror*. Well, here it was. Lesley stared at the new her for a long time.

"When in Rome, do as the Romans do," said Noah in her head.

Yeah, okay. But what about "To thine own self be true?"

What was her real self? The Canadian one—or this? She no longer knew.

Getting Used to Things

"You look Shula! Shula good worker. Not lazy. You work like Shula."

Lesley was sprawled on one of the kibbutz lawns under a shady tree, while Shula, a few yards away, was struggling to start a motor mower with an engine like an outboard motorboat's. Every time she pulled on the rope, it gave a few strangled coughs, and died.

"But it won't start," said Lesley. "I might as well rest till—"

The head gardener, a middle-aged man called Moshe who talked bad English with a strong Hungarian accent, would accept no such feeble excuses. His gardens were his life, and besides, he had a serious down on youthful shirking.

"You come with me! Find for you job, no problem!" he said, beckoning her with a grimy finger.

Shula looked up from her task and saw Lesley struggling, bottom first, to her feet. It wasn't a particularly hot day—it was still winter—but for Lesley, any work made her feel as if it were midsummer. Every half hour or so, she just seemed to have to collapse.

Shula said something to Moshe in Hebrew. Moshe made grumbling noises, but he said, "Okay, Shula say she need you. I come back later," he threatened. "No lazy. No sit. *Beseder?*"

"*Beseder,*" agreed Lesley wearily. As soon as Moshe was out of sight, she groaned and fell flat on her back on the lawn, but as a joke this time. Shula laughed.

"Working in the *noi* is easy or more harder than kitchen?"

"Nothing's worse than the kitchen," said Lesley emphatically.

"You were like better the *lul*?" teased Shula.

By now Lesley knew the names of all the different branches of the kibbutz where the kids did a work stint after school. There was the *refet,* where her father worked—that was the cowshed. (*Can you believe it?* she wrote to Noah in one of her secret letters. *Dad up to his knees in cow muck, and claiming he loves it?*) The *lul* was the chicken house. She'd worked there at first. Awful. Long, long sheds full of dust, stink, and a million hens, pecking at her fiercely when she had to reach under them for their eggs, and the huge white cockerels that scared her to death by attacking her from the rear. She hadn't lasted a week in the *lul*.

72

Her mother had been assigned to the *mitbakh,* the enormous communal kitchens. After the fiasco with the *lul,* they'd put Lesley in there, too.

"What's it like, Mom?" Lesley had asked apprehensively. She'd begun to think all kinds of work were beyond her.

Her mother had been noncommittal. The *work* was easy enough, she said, as if there were more to it than that. But Lesley soon found out it wasn't easy for her. She simply didn't know how her mother stuck it. The heat, the steam, the noise, the mountains of food which meant that each chore was endless, and the constant smells of their funny cooking . . . horrible! Once, when she'd had to dip about a thousand chicken pieces into some disgusting yellow stuff and lay them in deep friers, like huge metal boxes, with the heat coming up off the fat, she'd had to run out and throw up. After that, the work manager (who didn't hide the fact that he was getting heartily fed up with her) had moved her yet again.

Now here she was working with Shula in the *noi*—the gardens. It was nice to be outdoors; at least there were no awful smells and people (or hens) rushing frantically about, but the garden work was hard. They had to weed and dig and spray and lay new lawns (a terrible business, involving a lot of bending) and mow the old ones. That's what they were meant to be doing now. Only the mower was old and stubborn and had a mind of its own. It was the curse of their lives.

With her powerful right arm, Shula finally forced the ancient motor into life, and the machine started juddering away by itself before they could grab hold of the handle.

They rushed to catch up with it, turned it, and forced it up to the top of a slope—it was incredibly heavy and awkward—but before they could heave it onto the flat, it had somehow started down again—backward.

Lesley, when she felt it bearing down on her, abandoned her half of the wide handle and leaped out of the way.

"Les-lee!" shrieked Shula, battling to keep the horrible thing from running her over. Lesley dithered, but before she could do anything, Shula had regained control and put the brake on.

Lesley trailed back sheepishly. She was sure Shula would be mad at her—she'd really chickened out—but instead Shula just cursed the mower. Her father was an English Cockney who used all sorts of slang and swearing in his English, which he spoke to Shula's mother, not intending Shula to understand; but she picked up more than she was supposed to.

"I am *hating* this damn *mikasakhat*! Why it go the hell *akhora* when I want that it go *kadima*?"

Akhora—kadima . . . Backward. Forward. Obvious, when the new words were embedded in English sentences, even Shula's funny ones. Lesley was picking up Hebrew words without effort, at least while she worked with Shula. But that wasn't helping her in class.

Lesley had always taken success for granted. Now she was not successful in anything. She was hopeless at work, in a community where all prestige was based on how well you did your job. She might have shone in sports, but winter was the season for football, not basketball.

And school was sheer, unmitigated agony.

If she had felt frustrated in the classes at the center, how much worse was it now, sitting with kids of her own age, kids among whom—sooner or later—she *had* to earn a place. All day long she sat beside Shula, keeping her back very straight and her eyes fixed on Meir, their teacher, struggling with all her might to grasp and to follow . . . struggling not to cry because she couldn't. Occasionally she couldn't help herself: the hopeless frustration was too much, and the tears just ran silently down her cheeks. Everyone, including Shula, pretended not to notice.

Meir took her aside. He spoke a little English and was very nice.

"You like I arrange special Hebrew lessons?"

He picked a bad time to ask. It had been a ghastly morning. Lesley couldn't even speak, she was so upset. She just bit hard on the inside of her lips and shook her head.

The main thing that kept her going was music.

Music was a big thing here. A lot of the kids played in the youth orchestra. The music teacher asked her if she'd like to learn the recorder. At first she refused. She just didn't have the confidence. But Shula said, "Music is good, recorder is easy. Why you don't try?" So without much hope, Lesley tried.

The others were mostly onto "real" instruments by now, but Ofer—who played the oboe—was told to help her. She found she loved it. It gave her comfort. When she couldn't talk to anyone, she could always practice. And when, after a few weeks, Ofer said, "You play good," it was balm to her soul.

But Ofer was not a friend. He was just a boy she shared

a bedroom with! (This turned out not to be so bad. There was a rule you had to turn your back when anyone in the room asked. It wasn't what you could call privacy, but Lesley got used to it; in fact, sharing had its advantages.)

Only Shula made a serious effort to befriend her—Shula whom at first Lesley had looked down on, Shula the fat, the frizzy, the pudding-faced, but who turned out to be one of the most popular people in the group because she was such fun, such a good sport, prepared to turn her hand to anything. Now she turned it to Lesley.

It was Shula whose strong hands kneaded the aches out of Lesley's back after she'd practically broken it laying a lawn. Shula who made her laugh with her funny English and her clowning. Shula who didn't wait to be asked, but came right up to her after lessons and said, "I can to do crappy old *avodat-bayit* with you?"

Avodat-bayit was homework, and even with Shula's help there wasn't much of it Lesley could do at first. But math wasn't so impossible—thank heaven for figures! They, like musical notes, at least stayed the same. Shula wasn't too hot on math. Lesley was able to help her, for a change.

But Shula, for all her kindness and funniness, couldn't bridge the gap between not belonging and belonging. Now that Lesley's novelty had worn off, the others tended to leave her to herself. It didn't occur to her that they were embarrassed at not being able to talk to her properly. In her newfound insecurity, she thought they disliked her. So she assumed a poised, faintly contemptuous manner, as if she couldn't care less. Then they gave her a nickname, which she overheard.

76

"What's '*snobbeet*'?" she asked Shula. Shula put her nose in the air and flicked her forefinger under it. "You mean, stuck-up? But I'm not!"

Shula could only shrug. "*I* know it," she said. Lesley felt crushed. She had never felt crushed like that in her whole life before.

She went home for "four-o'clock meal" that day in such a black mood of misery that her parents couldn't ignore it.

"What's the matter, bubba?" asked her father. He was slumped in the one armchair looking exhausted. He nearly always did, these days. His waistline was going back to normal; in fact, his clothes (Lesley still hadn't got used to seeing him dressed like a farmer—his shoes weren't polished now!) seemed to hang on him. So did the skin around his jaw.

"Nothing, Daddy."

"Not much!" He pushed himself into a more upright position in the chair, and she noticed a grimace pass over his face.

"What's the matter with *you*?" she asked. "Are you hurting?"

"Just my back. It's those straw bales . . . forking them off the truck . . . it's nothing."

"Not much!" she retorted in her turn. "Why don't you lie down on your bed and I'll rub your back? Shula does it for me."

"Nonsense—rubbish," began her father. But her mother came straight in off the porch where she'd been making tea, headed directly for her husband, hiked him up without a word, and led him, protesting in vain, to the bed.

The mere sight of it seemed to rob him of all resistance. He flopped onto it on his face with a groan.

Lesley lifted his legs straight and said capably, "Okay, just relax." She leaned over him and began to massage his shoulder blades.

"It's farther down," he mumbled. "Ah. Yes. There. Unnghhh . . . Fantasticorum . . . pepsicolum . . . Oof! You're really getting to it . . . it feels . . . just too pistachiolarious. . . ."

Lesley couldn't help laughing. She couldn't stay sunk in her misery when her dad started his nonsense talk. It seemed years since he'd done any.

"Fantasticorum, is it? Say, you'll have to show me this new therapy of Shula's," remarked her mother. She was wheeling in the tea trolley she'd laid, out on the porch. She invariably set it out nicely with teacups and tea in a pot, little plates, and larger plates full of sliced homemade cake, bread and butter, jam, cheese, and sometimes sliced tomatoes or mashed hard-boiled egg to make sandwiches. It was kind of like a kids' birthday party, every day.

At the beginning, Lesley had protested.

"Mom, you don't have to do all this. What's it all about anyway?"

"It's the custom here," she replied. "In England they call it having tea. Anyway, it's the only time we're all together. I like to prepare food for you both, it's like old times."

It wasn't that Lesley actually minded having a nice four o'clock meal. She was usually quite hungry after her two-hour stint in the garden, her after-work shower, and brief siesta. But something bothered her about it, and one day she'd found out what.

She'd come home to find both her parents flat out on the bed, fast asleep. She'd quietly drawn the curtain that divided the two rooms, grabbed a handful of breadsticks and a glass of milk, and lain down on the rug with a book. It had been nice . . . more normal, like at Shula's, with nobody making a fuss.

Suddenly her mother had "come to," leaped off the bed, and started rushing about, "looking after her," apologizing for having overslept. . . . That was when Lesley realized for the first time how terribly tired they both were. On top of working six hours a day in that dreadful kitchen, her mother had to come home, clean up the apartment, bake cake, and make sandwiches. . . . Lesley wished she wouldn't.

Now her mother was saying, "Would you like a cheese sandwich? Or tomato? I'll make it for you." She was pouring tea from the pot, concentrating, not looking at anyone. Lesley, rubbing and kneading her father's aching back, suddenly remembered the words from Noah's letter: "As to Mom, I'm frankly worried. . . ."

"Are you okay, Mom?"

"Sure I am! I'm fine and dandy. Come get your tea. I made orange cake today."

On impulse, Lesley left her father and went to her mother. She put her arm around her and kissed her. Instead of smiling at her, her mother turned her face away as if there were something in it that she didn't want Lesley to see. This worried Lesley so much that she forgot about the kids calling her *snobbeet,* at least till she got back to the *kitta.*

Then she remembered. And more particularly because it was *p'oola* night.

There was almost always some activity going on in *kitta,* usually a noise-making one: the radio or the record player blaring, kids shouting back and forth, Ofer practicing his oboe in the room, people banging in and out through the screen door. There were meetings of various committees—elected groups for settling disputes, arranging outings, choosing films, and thrashing out work rotas and school problems. There was orchestra practice and various other rehearsals from time to time—lots of things for Lesley to feel left out of.

But the *p'oolot* were different. They were something secret. That made it worse somehow.

It happened about once a fortnight. The others would all put on bright blue shirts with a thick white lace crisscrossing at the neck, and disappear into the darkness outside, to return several hours later flushed and chattering. They made a great point of shushing, fingers to lips, whenever she was anywhere about—as if she could understand a word. This we're-inside-you're-outside attitude made Lesley sore.

Shula tried to help.

"You want to know where we go?"

Lesley desperately did. But she just tossed her head.

"Is big secret only everybody know. *P'oolot.* You know what is a *p'oola*? When soldier go out and—" She mimed firing a rifle.

"An attack? Do you all go out and attack someone in your little blue shirts?"

"Not go bang-bang. We go out and do things. It is for *t'nua.*"

With Shula's help, Lesley looked up both words in her Hebrew-English dictionary. *P'oola* was "an action, often military" and *t'nua* was "a political movement." She was more bewildered than ever.

"What 'political movement'?"

"We are call Young Guards."

"Is it like Scouts and Guides?"

"No!" said Shula scornfully. "Scouts is not politics."

"What politics?"

"We are *Socialistim*," said Shula proudly.

Lesley knew her parents were long-time Socialists. That was part of what had brought them here, where Socialism was a reality that people actually tried to live by, not just an ideal.

"Okay, but what about these 'actions'? What do you do?"

"Lots. Sometimes we go out with the little kids in the night and teach them nature and play games. I am *madrikha*," she said proudly.

The dictionary again. It meant a youth leader.

"Okay," Lesley said again. "Tell me more."

But Shula couldn't—or wouldn't.

That evening, when Lesley came back from her parents', she saw some of the kids in their blue shirts and her heart sank. But then Shula came bursting out to meet her, her round face flushed.

"Our *madrikh* say, you want to come on a *p'oola* with us?"

For just a moment, Lesley's spirits lifted. But then she thought, *No, why should I, they don't really want me, they don't like me.* And I don't like them.

So she said aloofly, "Oh, no thanks. It all sounds rather babyish."

Shula's face fell. She turned and went back through the screen door without another word.

Arabs

Early on, while Lesley was still completely out of her depth and hating the kibbutz and practically everything in it, she left it one Sabbath morning through the main gate (locked and guarded at night, but open all day) determined to make her way down to the river.

She was missing her own river. It had become a symbol for her of all she'd left behind. At that time she was writing regular letters, not just to Noah but to Sonia, Lee, and even Auntie Hannah. . . . All she dreamed of was getting home.

That morning she had the dim idea that being close to this river—the legendary Jordan—would soothe her mind and help her to feel closer to her own, lost one. But to her great disappointment, before she could even approach the bank and see what the river looked like, a kibbutznik suddenly appeared—giving her a great fright—and asked her what she was doing there.

"I want to get down to the river," she said.

"No you don't," he said firmly. He turned her around and gave her a little push back along the road to the kibbutz.

"But why not?" she asked over her shoulder.

All he did was wag his finger warningly and say, *"Oy-va-voy!"* which she knew meant "Don't be naughty or there'll be trouble."

She told Shula. Shula laughed and said, "Stupid! The river is *gvul* between us and them. Sometimes we go but we not suppose. You want to see river? Come, I show you."

She led her, not toward the river, but up a hill in the middle of the kibbutz, which overlooked all the surrounding countryside. At the top was a large, rounded building. Shula led her up some outside steps and onto a balcony. They walked around it to the side facing the pink hills of Jordan, and Shula pointed.

"There is river Jordan."

"Where?" asked Lesley, looking.

"There. See the shine?"

Lesley stared. That? That narrow glinting bit of water between steep banks of scrub and trees? It looked like a little pond.

"But the song says 'deep river'!" she exclaimed. "I thought it would be big, like the river at home!"

Shula shrugged. "Is small, and then we make more small, take water from it for our *hashka'a* and other thing," she said. "They take, too." She pointed across to the other side.

Lesley was trying to pick out the path of the river from the greenery that grew on its banks. It seemed to twist like a snake in loops between the green fields of the kibbutz and the barren-looking land of the Arabs.

"Why is ours so green and theirs so brown?"

"Poor farmers. Not have tractor. Not do *hashka'a*." Several boys in the class, including Ofer, worked in *hashka'a*—irrigation. It was very important for the kibbutz crops. "We have pump. See it—little box, there? They must to take water from the river without pump. But they do pretty good. See? That green, that their *pardess*." She pointed to a square clump of dark green, right on the edge of the river—an orange grove.

Suddenly Shula clutched her arm. "Look there!"

Lesley looked, and saw a man, a boy, and a donkey coming along a track that led alongside the river on the far side. They were about three hundred yards away. The donkey was laden with boxes. The man, wearing a black robe and white headdress, walked ahead, and the boy walked behind, occasionally speeding the donkey with a whack from a long stick. He looked about ten.

The girls watched until they disappeared into the orange trees.

"Why does he hit it all the time?"

"Every *Arabush* do. Automatic."

"*Arabush*? I thought the Hebrew for Arabs was *Aravim*."

Shula looked embarrassed. "It's a not-nice name for them."

"You mean, like saying 'Yids' for Jews?"

Shula didn't answer. She was biting her fingernails, a bad habit she had.

"Do you hate them?" Lesley asked.

"Me? I don't hate nothing."

"But they hate us?" It was the first time Lesley had ever said "us" meaning "us Israelis." It just slipped out, but she felt a pang of disloyalty to Canada and hastily corrected herself: "I mean, you."

"They fright of us."

"Just that?"

"Angry, too. They think we stole land of them."

"But we didn't. You didn't."

"*Betakh sh'lo*. We buy it. Million-million of money to the *Aravim*. Then in the war of forty and eight, they come against us, and we win them, and get more land. From then they don't leave us no peace. Always the terrorist come. Put bombs. Kill people."

"Here? Do they come around here?"

She shook her head.

"So why do we need the fence?" asked Lesley, pointing.

"You can never know when they will start with us," said Shula. "You can never—believe them."

"Trust them."

"Right."

They stood together, staring at the river, so narrow, little more than a stream, that lay between them and the enemy.

"Are you ever 'fright'?" asked Lesley.

Shula looked up at her and gave her a little grin.

"My brother Rami say we don't be fright, never," she said. "Our army take care on us."

That was many weeks ago now. But Lesley liked to go up onto the balcony of the big building—which was called the culture house, where they sometimes had visiting orchestras or theater companies—and stare out across the tiny river.

She would sing under her breath "Deep River," or the other spiritual she'd thought of:

> One more river, and that's the river of Jordan—
> One more river, there's one more river to cross.

There were several Arab villages within sight—patchworks of bleached stone boxes with networks of fields, groves, and vineyards around them, and little thready tracks, leading away. It was down one of these that the Arab and his son and donkey came to work. Because they were the closest, Lesley took more interest in them than in the others she sometimes saw, pursuing their lives further off.

She liked the donkey, and called him Eeyore in her thoughts. But she didn't like the boy. He kept hitting the donkey. It made Lesley wince. In her head, she told him to stop, and had other pretend conversations with him. But of course she knew he wouldn't understand, even if they could possibly meet face to face.

But then, at the beginning of the spring term, Meir made

an announcement that drew groans from the class, but made Lesley sit up.

"Tomorrow your Arabic teacher is coming to begin your course."

"Why the four winds do we have to learn *Arabic*?" grumbled several of the kids.

"We share this country, and geographically we're part of the Arab world. Many things divide us. Language shouldn't be one of them."

"But the language of Israel is Hebrew!" objected Yossi. "Let them learn *Ivrit*."

Meir smiled. "They do," he said. "You should speak their language half as well as most of them speak ours."

Their Arab teacher was a man from a local village. It was the first time Lesley had known that there were Arab villages within Israel. Meir told them that one in six Israeli citizens was an Arab. Lesley wasn't the only one who was surprised at that. The class burst into discussion.

Arabs—Israeli citizens? With the same rights?

"Yes," said Meir firmly, "and one of them is to be treated with respect. Don't you ever let me hear you're giving Akhmed a hard time."

Akhmed came. Another surprise. He didn't dress in a long robe and a white headdress; he wore ordinary trousers and a sweater. He was nice-looking and spoke excellent Hebrew. But it didn't take the class long to find out he wasn't a very good teacher. He seemed nervous and unsure. Some kids began to play him up. It was the usual bunch—Amnon, Yossi, and Gadi, in particular—but some of the girls egged them on by giggling. The lessons were full of tension. Not much was learned.

88

Lesley watched, and judged. She felt embarrassed for Akhmed, and a bit ashamed of the way some of the kids behaved. Besides, she was keen on this new subject. With it they were all on the same level, and Lesley thought, "In this, at least, I can beat them."

So, although she was still struggling with Hebrew, she worked like mad. Soon she was the best in the class in Arabic. Akhmed smiled at her shyly when she answered well.

One day, when he did this, Gadi hissed at her under his breath, "Why don't you just kiss him!"

Lesley hissed back, *"Shtok!"* which was a rude way of saying "shut up."

"Since you like Arabs so much," he whispered (Akhmed was writing on the board), "with your *wonderful* Arabic you can move to the village and live in their dirt!"

Akhmed heard. He turned sharply, his face flushed.

"Gadi, please don't be offensive," he said in his good Hebrew.

" 'Please don't be offensive'!" mimicked Gadi. "She's offensive. She speaks better Arabic than Ivrit. All she knows in Ivrit is *'shtok'*!"

Outrage—and her sense of outsiderhood—boiled up inside Lesley. Her face flamed and her temper snapped. Without stopping a moment to think, she slammed out of the class and went straight to Meir. Filled with self-righteousness, she reported the conversation exactly.

Meir was furious, something very rare for him. That evening he called the whole class together and gave them a piece of his mind.

"Be ashamed to be so rude—so inhospitable! If you ever

went to Akhmed's village—and he's invited you, only I don't think you're ready—he'd teach you how to receive guests. 'Dirt' indeed—I've seen more dirt in this *kitta* than in Akhmed's home! Gadi, you make me ashamed. It's against everything the kibbutz stands for. Have I in my class one little racist?"

Gadi hung his head for once, but whether it did him any good in the long run was questionable. It certainly didn't do Lesley any.

She found out how bad it is to live, work, eat, and learn with eighteen people who are not speaking to you. Even Shula didn't. The very worst was working with her in the *noi* in silence.

After three dreadful days of it, Lesley suddenly threw down her hoe and turned on Shula. "Call yourself a friend! You're behaving like a real mean pig! How would you like it?"

"I would not to do it."

"Do what? What d'you mean?"

Shula opened and shut her mouth, and then said, "I tell you tonight. When I go home, I ask my father for the word."

She came back with it that evening.

"Is not done to snitch."

" 'Is not done' to talk like Gadi did!"

"Right. That don't make it okay to snitch. What you should, after lesson you just give it to Gadi on his head, and finish."

"Okay, I didn't know. Are you going to go on not talking to me?"

Shula looked uncomfortable, shrugged, bit her nail, and walked away.

This was the lowest Lesley had fallen since they came to the kibbutz.

Half of her didn't want to even go to Arabic lessons anymore. But the stubborn part took over. She gritted her teeth and tried harder than ever. If she neglected anything, it was Hebrew—what was the point when no one was talking to her?

One day Lesley borrowed a pair of army field glasses from Shula's brother Rami, who had just finished basic training in the army, and went up to the culture house balcony.

She was deeply unhappy. The kids were still punishing her. She couldn't even tell her parents, and as for Meir, if he noticed, he said nothing. Kids were supposed to be self-reliant. . . . Lesley was hating them all; all kibbutzniks were rotten. Okay, so she would be interested in their enemies.

When she saw the tiny approaching figures of the boy and his father and the donkey, she trained the glasses on them, her heart, for some reason, beginning to pound. The man wore broken shoes under his long black dress-like garment. He had a hard expression and a black mustache. But she wasn't very interested in him. It was the little boy and the donkey she wanted to look at.

When she turned the glasses onto the little boy, she was amazed to see that he was not as young as she'd thought. He was very thin and short, but he was old-faced. It was hard to guess his age, but he might be even a little older than she was.

His expression was set and sour as he scuffed along through the dust behind the donkey. Suddenly, on impulse it seemed, he took a running jump and leapfrogged onto the donkey's rump. Startled, it took a few trotting steps and bumped into the man in front. He turned angrily, saw the boy, and with one swipe of his hand, knocked him off.

Lesley watched him pick himself up. He resumed his place behind the donkey, and gave it a kick. For once, Lesley understood. He couldn't kick his father, so he kicked the animal.

Lesley whispered under her breath, "Don't hurt Eeyore; it's not his fault." Then she realized she could say so much in Arabic, and began a little "conversation" which, if the boy could have heard it, he might have understood.

"My name is Lesley. What's your name?"

She made him answer with the name of the boy in the Arab textbook: Mustapha. She practiced her Arabic on him until, unaware of being watched, the trio trudged out of sight.

After that she often escaped from her miserable situation into the small life of Mustapha and Eeyore. She wrote about them in her diary, as a break from writing about how mean the others were. Rami got quite curious about why she was borrowing his binoculars so often.

One evening Lesley hurried to the *kitta* and unlocked her box. Something had happened that she wanted to write down—something really interesting.

Mustapha and his father were working late. They were out of sight among the orange trees. I had the glasses trained on Eeyore standing by himself at the top of the bank. I expect he was thirsty, because suddenly he started to try to get down to the river. That rotten Mustapha always hobbles his forelegs so tight he had to make a little sort of jump with them every forward step, and suddenly he tripped and fell.

My heart was in my mouth! He slipped and rolled down the bank and into the shallow water at the edge. He brayed with fright, and Mustapha came bursting out of the trees, waving his stick and shouting at poor Eeyore, who couldn't get up.

Mustapha ran down to him and started to drag on the halter rope with one hand, beating poor Eeyore as hard as he could with the other. I thought I could hear him cursing. Eeyore just couldn't make it with the hobble on, and at last Mustapha had to untie him, and then of course dear, good, willing Eeyore scrambled up at once. That stinking Mustapha just started beating him in a frenzy.

It made me sick to see him! Suddenly I just lost my temper and shouted at the top of my voice, "Let him alone, you pig!"

He heard me! He stopped and looked around. I was wearing my white shirt and I waved both arms to catch his eye and shouted again, "Stop beating him! Stop—beating —him!" Of course, I was shouting in English, but then I remembered the Arabic for "stop" and yelled it out.

Suddenly he saw me. He had the stick raised in his hand and he didn't know what to do. We just stood there, a long way apart, silent and staring at each other. I had a sudden urge to wave! I was just going to when I heard someone calling me from below, close. I looked down, and there was Meir, standing under the balcony, looking up at me with a puzzled face.

"Who are you shouting at?" he asked. "An Arab boy across the river, he's beating his donkey." Meir looked amazed. "Did he hear you?" "Yes. He's looking straight at me this minute."

Meir started up the steps. "Come away, come down!" I didn't move. When he reached me I wanted to show him Mustapha and explain, but he didn't give me time. He took my arm and hustled me down to the ground.

"But why?" I asked. "Because you mustn't shout at the Arabs. What's it your business what he does with his donkey? It's no use trying to be in touch with them."

This was strange coming from Meir, who's always telling us we ought to get on with them. I set off as if I was going back to the kitta, but when Meir was out of sight, I raced back to the culture house. But by the time I got back, it was nearly dark, and of course they'd gone.

T E N

A Two-Way View

There was a girl in the class called Esther whom Lesley admired and envied. She was what Lesley had been, in Saskatoon: the acknowledged class leader. She was always that bit more daring and with it than the rest. She was also very bright in school—at everything but English.

So when she came to Lesley one day with a proposition, Lesley paid very close attention.

"I want to make friends with the visitors. I want to understand the movies. My English stinks. You help me and I'll help you."

This was the blunt *sabra* approach. They all talked like that, so Lesley wasn't offended. What she saw here was a chance to get off the

95

blacklist she'd been on since she'd snitched on Gadi. She said, "Okay. What's the problem?"

Esther switched to English. "For example. Why we must to say, 'I have done it' and not 'I did it'? I don't see!"

"First off, we don't say 'to' after 'must.'"

"We don't?"

"No. As to 'have done' and 'did'. . . . Let me think." Lesley frowned, trying to formulate a rule. "'Have done' is if you've *just* done something."

"But that's still the past. Why it's called '*present* perfect tense'?"

Lesley said, "I'll tell you tomorrow."

She did some thinking, and asking. The next day she said, "'Perfect' means 'finished.' The action is finished in the present."

They were sitting in the classroom waiting for the teacher to come. The others were crowding around. They were all having trouble with the present perfect tense.

"Give me example."

Lesley gave them one she'd already thought of.

The whole class burst out laughing. "Say it again, Leslee!" And when their English teacher arrived in the class, she was greeted with a rousing chorus:

"Poosy–cat, poosy–cat, where have you *been*?
I've *been* up to *Lon*-don to *vee*-seet the *Queen*!"

"Very good!" she said. "Where did you learn that?"

"Leslee teached us!"

Afterward Esther said, "You're a good teacher. Better than our real one. You want to be on the culture commit-

96

tee with me? You can maybe teach us English songs to do at Purim."

A few nights later, Lesley came into the bedroom. Shula was already lying down with her little light off. Ofer was cleaning his oboe. Aviva was out at choir practice.

Lesley said, "Ofer, *tistovev*—turn your back."

"Oh . . . ! I won't look. Anyway," he noticed, "you're already in your pajamas."

"It's the rule you have to turn your back if I ask you," said Lesley.

Ofer sighed heavily and turned, still fiddling with his oboe. Lesley stooped quickly and got the locket out of the mattress. She opened it, took out the key, and unlocked her box.

"What have you got in there, anyhow?"

She spun around, but Ofer still had his back dutifully turned.

"My own things."

"Secrets?"

"So what?"

"Letters from your Arab boyfriend?"

Lesley gaped. "What?"

"Think we don't know about him?" he said. "You're crazy."

"Don't be stupid."

"I've heard you stand up on the culture house balcony and signal to him."

Lesley's heart jumped. Signal? Could anyone think that? A signal sounded sort of—military.

"I don't signal! Once I waved."

Ofer said again, "You're *meshuggah.*"

"I don't see why."

"You don't see nothing. They're Arabs."

"So's Akhmed an Arab."

"He's one of our Arabs. The ones over there are different. They're all *kharar.*"

Lesley was shocked. It wasn't like Ofer to swear. She said primly, "Meir says it's not nice to say stuff like that."

"So run and tell him."

Lesley felt a real pang. Things had started to ease up. Gadi still didn't speak to her, and she didn't care, but for Ofer to still get at her, hurt.

She took her box into the classroom, which was empty but for David, the class dunce, struggling with his homework. She settled down to write to Noah—she wrote to him regularly, though she never got a reply—but she had hardly started when she heard running feet.

"Listen what's happened!" she heard Aviva shouting. "Come and hear!"

The *kitta* came to life. Kids who were getting ready for bed came running out of their rooms half-dressed. Danny emerged from the showers with a towel around him, dripping wet. Others, like Shula, who'd been asleep rolled out of bed and into the corridor. David dropped his book happily and dashed out of the classroom, with Lesley hot on his heels.

They all crowded around Aviva, who was bursting with news. She started to pour it out in a rapid flow of Hebrew. Lesley struggled to follow, but soon had to turn to Shula for help.

"What is it? What's happened?"

"*Aravim* cross the river!" she stuttered, putting her fingernails between her teeth.

"What do you mean? Their army?"

"No, no—just some silly clots come to pinch."

"Were they caught?"

"No. But Aviva see them running away. One have a—*off*—brk-brk—" She made noises like a hen. "One grab stuff from the porch of somebody."

"But how did they cross the river?"

Shula shrugged her fat shoulders. "Is not deep."

"Has it happened before?"

"Sure. You know what I think. I think it's just young kids. Like a game."

"We used to play that in Canada. We called it Truth or Dare."

"Safer in Canada. Here you can get dead from it."

Suddenly Lesley thought of something. She seized Aviva, who was still excitedly answering questions.

"Which houses did they go to?"

"The ones facing the river."

A wave of alarm washed over Lesley. Her parents' house faced the river. She ran out in her pajamas.

The kibbutz was well lit at night, but still it was a bit scary. The bushes that bordered the narrow paths were dense in places, enough to hide any number of prowlers. . . . She shivered as she passed the last "streetlamp" and had to face a dark patch of lawn; but she could see the back windows of her parents' rooms lit up in streaks through the closed shutters. She took a breath and bolted across and around the end of the building.

Something had certainly happened. She could hear a lot

of voices from the main room, all talking at once. As she entered the porch, she saw a jug of milk smashed on the tiles, and she at once spotted some little things missing: a soapstone Eskimo carving of a seal, a bright-colored egg timer. . . . She burst into the room.

"Mom—Daddy—are you okay?"

The room was full of excited people, mostly neighbors. The night watchman was there, with his Uzi under his arm, and then Lesley noticed an army officer and an ordinary soldier talking to her father.

Her mother came up to her and put her arms around her. Lesley felt embarrassed, as if they were all—herself included—overdramatizing the whole thing. After all—an egg timer! It seemed pretty trivial to be making all this fuss over.

But the soldiers evidently didn't think it was trivial at all. They were questioning her father about every detail. It seemed he and her mother had been fast asleep in bed (Lesley had a sense of astonishment that her parents went to bed before her!) when they'd been disturbed by a noise from the porch. Her father had jumped out of bed and rushed out, turning on the light, in time to see a figure running toward the perimeter fence. He'd watched helplessly while the thief slipped underneath somehow and across the road, to disappear in the darkness toward the river.

"Why didn't you call out?" asked the officer.

"I don't know—I was so absorbed with watching him— he was very small, didn't look more than about ten—"

"What!" asked Lesley suddenly. It was out before she

100

could stop it. Everyone turned to look at her, and she put her hand over her mouth.

"Do you know anything about this?" the officer asked, fixing her with sharp, suspicious eyes.

"No, how could I? I was in the *kitta*," said Lesley innocently.

The interrogation went on. Lesley's mother made tea for everyone. Nobody else's porch had been robbed, it seemed, and what had been taken from the Shelbys' had been so trifling that at first Mrs. Shelby couldn't be sure anything was missing. Lesley pointed out the missing seal and egg timer, and the officer made a solemn note of them.

They had just decided that that was it when Lesley's father suddenly said, "Hey, Miriam—where's Lesley's picture?"

They looked. There had been a photo of Lesley tacked to the doorjamb. It was gone—torn off the tack.

"What on earth would anyone want that for?" Lesley said. "I looked just awful in it!"

Everyone burst out laughing then: all except the officer. He was looking at Lesley in that funny way she didn't care for at all.

The next day after work, Lesley went back to the *kitta* to shower and change. She was absolutely dying to go up to the culture house balcony to see if she could see Mustapha, but she'd had such a fright the night before that she didn't dare.

She sat there brooding. The idea of crossing the river, either way, had never occurred to her since that first day, when Ayala had explained that it was the border. Despite the openness of the countryside, the ease with which you could almost wade across, that had made it seem impossible.

But Mustapha had crossed!—if it was him. Maybe Shula was right, and it was some kind of initiation test, or . . . But any other idea was too crazy. Even if Mustapha had wanted to see her, he couldn't have expected to. As for stealing her picture, that must have been just by chance. How could he know which was her parents' house?

Lesley had her diary on her knee, but she didn't write in it. Instead, she locked it away carefully and strolled outside.

The sun was warm and the kibbutz was looking beautiful. There'd been some rain. All the lawns were spring-green and there were wildflowers growing in the places Moshe the gardener had left uncultivated. The most beautiful were the wild red anemones; she sang to herself the song about them that was all the current rage:

"Calaniot . . . calaniot . . ."

Baruch, a boy in the class who was into history, had told them that *"calaniot"* had been the Jews' nickname for the British soldiers in the time before the State, because they wore red berets, red like the flowers. Lesley listened to the birds and thought how quiet and peaceful it was here. What must it have been like to live in Israel during that bad but exciting time, the time when the Jews were fighting the British and then fighting the Arabs?

The flowers were a protected species; you weren't supposed to pick them, but just a few wouldn't hurt. She picked three. She'd give them to her mother to put in the little finger-vase that a neighbor had given her for her birthday last week. That had been some terrific birthday. Lesley wondered if hers, when it came in August, would be so happy. The kitchen had made her mother a marvelous cake and given her a bottle of wine to celebrate. People came with little gifts to wish her *mazal tov,* and Lesley noticed her mother's tense, anxious expression soften and a real old-times smile light up her tired face. She seemed to get more kick out of those cheap little presents than out of the grand things she'd always gotten at home. She'd practically gone crazy over Lesley's, which was a rather messy batik wall hanging she'd managed to make under Ruth's instruction (Ruth was the class artist). Lesley hadn't given her mother a handmade present for years. . . . Thinking about that made Lesley feel better.

On the way to her parents', she couldn't resist a detour to the culture house. Dare she? She looked around in all directions. There was no one about. She mounted the steps quickly and squinted out across the burgeoning, sunny landscape. Suddenly she caught her breath.

It was him!—a tiny figure in the distance. He was sitting—she could just make him out—on the top of the far bank. But the weird thing was, he was wearing a mask; at least, that was what it looked like—a black strip across his eyes like a highwayman, and his hands were up on either side of his face, as if—

Lesley sucked in her breath, then shot down the steps and ran like the wind to the flat Rami shared with another soldier. She knocked, panting.

Rami, tall, bronzed, and with hair wet from the shower, came onto the porch.

"Nu?"

"Can I borrow your field glasses?"

"Again? What for?"

"To see something."

"What do you say!" he said sarcastically. He took them from a nail on the wall and handed them to her. "Here. Back tonight, okay?"

"Of course! Thanks a lot."

Rami went back in. But to Lesley's dismay, as he did, who should come out but Shula. She must have been visiting him.

"I know why you want those."

"You do not!"

"I yes do. To look your boyfriend across the river."

"Stop calling him that!" said Lesley furiously.

"I make a joke. But you must to be careful."

Lesley took her arm and pulled her out of earshot. "Come and look what he's doing!"

But when they got back to the balcony, the far bank was empty.

"He was there. He was looking through binoculars!"

Shula gaped at her. "No possible. From where a poor Arab boy get *mishkefot?*"

"I don't know! Listen, Shula. If I tell you something, will you promise and swear never to tell?"

"Yes."

"Cross your heart and hope to die and have to eat a dead pig's eye?"

"What you said?"

"That's how we swear."

"Stupid. I swear by the *kavod* of a Young Guard."

Kavod meant "honor."

"All right. Now listen. I think it was *him* who came last night."

Shula's round face was a study of incredulity. "Why you think so?"

"First I just had an idea. But I thought, why should he come *dafka* to my family's house? Only now I think he's been watching me, and look, he could see the house from there, with binoculars he could know which is my parents' house. So supposing he came and stole my picture?"

"You mean, he is gone on you?"

"Of course not!" Lesley said impatiently. "He'd just do it for a dare, like you said. Or maybe . . ." She stopped to think. "Listen, what if they have *p'oolot,* too? What if *he* belongs to some movement, like cadets or something, and they sent him across the river to prove he was brave enough to join?"

"From *them* maybe he gets the *mishkefot*—from the terrorists!" Shula's unbelief had turned to alarm.

Lesley knew quite enough to get an icy trickling feeling around the base of her skull.

"Listen, silly clot," Shula hissed. "You don't understand nothing. You think this is game. You forgot what Meir told us? How the young boys think the *terroristim* are so great they do anything to be with them? You think, not your problem, like all American visitors think—"

"I am not American!" Lesley answered fiercely. "And I'm not a visitor!"

105

The words were out before she'd stopped to think what they meant.

If she was not a visitor, what was she? Was she beginning to think of herself as just a little bit Israeli?

She rattled on, "I *do* understand, anyhow! I know how serious it is. I don't care anything about Mus—that Arab boy, why should I? I was just curious about him."

"So you not make bye-bye to him anymore or do silly thing?"

Lesley hesitated only a moment. "No."

"Or I must to snitch, like you."

"Okay already!"

"Cross your eye and hope to kill pig?"

Lesley burst into giggles. Shula started to laugh, too, and Lesley, with a huge sensation of relief, knew that they were friends again. She didn't swear, though, and Shula forgot to make her.

ELEVEN

The Challenge

But even without swearing, Lesley kept her promise. To tell the honest truth, some healthy fear was beginning to creep into her.

At first (Shula was right in a way) the whole situation in Israel with the Arabs had not seemed quite real to Lesley, because she had not grown up with it as the others had. When they talked about the "security situation" and terrorism, or she read about them in her dad's *Jerusalem Post,* it seemed—well, at a distance, somebody else's problem.

But after Shula had slyly compared her to an American visitor, she came to realize things had changed. She couldn't keep her distance anymore—not from Israel, not from the kibbutz, not from the others, and thus not from the "situation."

The things that affected the kibbutz and the kids she lived with had to affect her, too, because now she wanted to belong. When Ofer and Shula told her so seriously that she was crazy to have anything to do with the Arabs across the river, it stopped being a game. She didn't want them to have an excuse to say to her, "You don't understand." And although in her heart she could see no harm in watching, or even waving to, "Mustapha," something told her now that maybe he was not just—a boy. She couldn't quite bring herself to think of him as an enemy. But he was something "other." Something that just might be dangerous.

If she had just *thought* about all this, it might not have become clear to her what was happening to her, how her loyalties were changing. But she also wrote about it. She wrote in her diary, and she wrote to Noah. (Her letters to Sonia and Lee had petered out. It was hard even to picture them in her head anymore.)

Dearest Noah,

You see how faithfully I go on writing, even though I don't get letters back. I rack my brains how we could arrange something, but it's no use. Dad is finding this life harder than he expected, and although he'd die before admitting it, he is sort of "pulled" by the old life. Every day he goes up to the office and looks through the letters before the kibbutz secretary sorts them into the pigeonholes, hoping to find one from Saskatoon. He always asks who my (few!) letters are from. Sometimes I want to hear from you so much, I think I could tell lies, but I guess I couldn't, and maybe he'd find out anyhow. I shiver every time I think of him knowing I came to see you. Whatever it is he feels about what happened between you changes him somehow into something else.

Well, you told me things would get better if I worked on it. And you were right. Things are better, somehow. I'm not "in" yet, but I'm not completely out either. Tuesday we had a basketball game against kids from a neighboring kibbutz. Of course I'm not on the team, am I, so I nearly didn't go, but then Shula said, "Come on, stupid, and shout for our side," so I did. And right when we were losing 14–8, Aviva, that's my roommate, who was playing center, sprained her ankle, and David, he's the dumbo in our class but he's also the best athlete and the team captain, he just pulled me off the bench and said, "Play." Lucky I had my running shoes on. I guess I scored a few useful baskets and gave them all something to talk about. We didn't win, but we only lost by 3, and now it looks like I'm on the team!

Lessons aren't so ghastly now, either. My Ivrit (that's Hebrew to you!) is coming along. I guess when you hear it all day and need to talk to people, it just comes, and besides that, I'm having special lessons. . . . Then since Esther took me onto the culture committee and we started planning for pesach I had a few ideas, like we should do something with the very little kids, I mean some of our class have brothers and sisters that are just about old enough to come to the seder and they could take them up onstage and do the three questions with them, like in chorus, and I even composed a little tune on my recorder for it. This idea was passed on to

109

the adult committee and they liked it, so we're doing it. I had an idea for how we could do "the kid my father bought for two zuzim," but our class can only do one item, so maybe we'll do that next year. I'm already working on the tune, though.

Next year! Noah, what will be by next year? All anyone here can talk about is the "situation," which is getting bad (something about Egypt closing some waterway to our ships is the latest, have you heard about it?), but to be honest, all I can think about is, will I be a real part of the gang by then? Will my Hebrew be really good? Will I be better in school? Will they let me join the Movement and do p'oolot with the others?—I bet not. I bet they never will.

She was wrong.

One night, when the others were getting ready to go out on a *p'oola,* Esther came into Lesley's room in her brisk way and without a word put a parcel wrapped in crumpled brown paper on her bed.

"What's this?" Lesley asked.

"For you. Not to open till we've gone."

Lesley stood staring at the parcel. Since the night Shula had invited her to come on a *p'oola* and she had refused, she had always managed to be very busy on those special nights, pretended not to care where they went or that she was excluded. But she did care! Should she have swallowed her pride, and gone, that time? But in a dim way she sensed that, although for the wrong reason, she had done right. They didn't want her then. Only Boaz, their youth leader (who was much older, nearly ready for the army), had felt it his duty to include her.

110

Now perhaps it might be different.

She looked around at the other three. They all seemed very busy tying the laces of their blue shirts. Shula seemed to be struggling not to laugh.

"Come on. What's in it?"

"We don't know what it is," said Ofer with exaggerated innocence.

"Of course not. How should we?" said Shula.

Aviva looked at her watch importantly. "Come on, it's time."

They all said, "Shalom, Leslee!" as they left the room, and soon, with much banging of doors and shouting and laughing, they all left the building. Lesley was alone with the parcel.

It reminded her of something. Oh yes—the night her father had put the Shelby's boxes on her bed. It was a sort of trap, which she had duly fallen into. Was this another trap?

Curiosity overcame her. She fell on the parcel and ripped off the brown paper.

Inside, brand-new and stiffly starched, was a blue Movement shirt.

Not so long ago she would have hesitated, full of suspicion and doubt. Now she knew better. This was their way of saying what she had been aching for so long to hear: "We want you to be one of us."

In seconds she had stripped off her sweater and slipped the cool, stiff folds of the shirt over her head. She stood before the little mirror and her hands shook with excitement as she tied the white lace just so. She looked at herself. In a flash of insight she knew that she was happier to be

wearing this plain cotton shirt even than she'd been with
the dress with the Bonwit Teller label that she'd worn to
the junior dance. More proud of this than she had ever
been of being Lesley-the-Princess back home.

No. Not back home. Back in Saskatoon.

She gave herself a big, happy grin and dashed outside.

She'd expected them to be there, waiting for her, but
they weren't. For a moment she suffered a sharp pang of
anxiety. Could it be a mean joke, after all?

But suddenly she noticed a glow in the darkness. It was
an arrow, in red luminous paint, tacked to a tree. She ran
until she found the next arrow, and the next. The arrows
were leading her toward the perimeter of the kibbutz.

The next arrow was on the fence. It pointed straight to
the ground. Obediently, she lay flat and wriggled underneath, thinking with a little shiver that this might be the
very spot where Mustapha had escaped while her father
watched—Mustapha with her photo perhaps thrust into his
shirt, sticking to his sweating chest. Since the day after that,
she hadn't seen him. . . . For one brief second she allowed
herself to wonder about him.

She stood up on the road and looked all around. No
more arrows . . . But what had Shula said once? "Sometimes we go, but we not suppose. . . ." The river! At last
she would see the river! She looked left and right. All was
quiet. She crossed the road and began to run.

It was quite a long way through the scrub to where the
river was. Years ago her mother had made her join the
Guides. She had gone to camp once—just once, because
she had thought it boring and pointless to learn tracking

and get badges. Now she remembered how she'd been taught Indian skills: to slide your foot under the rustling leaves instead of plonking it down on top of them, to seek out a shadow and freeze if you heard a noise, how to turn your face down so it wouldn't reflect light and give you away.

After a while she saw a fire's glow through the trees. She crept closer. It was a small campfire burning in a little clearing. There was no one near it, or so she thought at first—but glancing quickly around, she saw a sudden flicker of white, then another, and another, and realized the wood was alive with tiny white snakes.

The snowy laces on the blue shirts!

They were moving in on her. She put on a sudden spurt and ran to the fire, reaching it just as the others burst into the clearing and fell on her.

"We didn't see you till the last!"

"You found the arrows?"

"You were so silent!"

They all kept their voices low. Then she noticed something else. The fire, which was small and neat, was built into a dug-out square of ground, and was screened from the side nearest the river by a double thickness of sacking between two stakes driven into the ground. This, and the thick foliage between them and the river, screened the fire from possible watchers on the far side.

"Where's Boaz?"

"He's not here tonight. It's just us."

"Is it dangerous here?" she asked.

"Oh, only a bit."

113

"Are we allowed?"

David grinned. The others didn't answer.

"Is this where you always come?"

They covered their mouths to suppress laughter.

"Of course not!" Shula giggled. "Tonight is special test for you."

"Have I passed?" Lesley asked confidently.

They all grew solemn. "Only the first part—the first test was finding us."

"You mean there's more tests?"

They all came and stood closely around her. David was the spokesman. Dunce he might be at lessons, but he was the tallest and toughest.

"You have three choices. *Aleph,* you can run all the way around the outer edge of the kibbutz. But if you are seen or challenged, you've failed. *Bet,* you can walk along the main road to the next kibbutz, which is three miles, and report to the *madrikh* there, and then walk back. You have to do it in one and a half hours, alone. *Gimmel—*"

He stopped. His face in the firelight was tense and flushed.

"I'm against," said Shula suddenly.

"You voted for," said David accusingly.

"I changed my opinion," said Shula.

"You can't, it's too late," said Naomi. She was the class daredevil, crazier and more daring than any of the boys. "I've done it. I did it before any of you. If I can, she can."

"Anyway," said Danny, "she's got a choice, she doesn't have to choose—*gimmel.*"

"What is it—what's *gimmel?*" asked Lesley, unable to bear the suspense.

"Well, it won't hurt to tell her," said David defensively. "So this is it." They drew in still closer together and his voice dropped to a whisper.

"About a kilometer downriver, there's a broken bridge. It's not in use, of course, and there's barbed wire at both ends, but you can easily climb up the legs of the bridge if you wade a little way into the water. What you have to do, if you choose *gimmel,* is take a piece of chalk and get onto the bridge and crawl halfway across, and in the middle you must make a mark. Then tomorrow morning we can stand on top of the bank and see you made it."

Lesley listened hard and then turned to Shula.

"I think I've got it, but tell me again in English."

Shula did. But she put a lot of stuff in about being quiet, being careful, not going one millimeter past the middle of the bridge. "And," she concluded, ever practical, "you have to roll your jeans legs right up and take off your shoes so Adda doesn't see you've been in the water. Or she might guess."

Adda was their *metapelet,* or housemother, who looked after their clothes and general welfare. She was a gentle, motherly woman, who seldom scolded them—many of the parents thought her far too easygoing. But just every now and then, if any of them misbehaved, she would get—not angry, but hurt. She could make you feel (as Yossi once said when she'd been after him) "like a real zero."

It would be terrible to have to face Adda, to hear her disappointed cry of "It hurts my heart," to know they had done something beyond the pale. The way Shula brought her into it made it suddenly crystal-clear to Lesley that this whole enterprise was utterly forbidden. If it were not, it

115

would hardly matter if Adda "guessed" where they'd been.

Lesley looked downward to the river. It crept past, glinting faintly; the other bank was just a blackness beyond the glimmer—but it was shockingly near.

From her perch on the culture house balcony, before she'd stopped going there, she'd often seen Arab patrols on the far side. Of course, that was in daytime. But wouldn't they take even more care at night? And what if their own soldiers should see her? She could imagine how someone like Shula's brother Rami—whom she had a secret crush on—could be very fierce and scathing, and could put you down so you'd never want to get up again.

Not to mention the sheer scariness of it. What if they mistook her for a terrorist, and shot her?

On the other hand, of all the three alternatives, *gimmel* was clearly her chance to prove herself as brave as the bravest of them, a chance she might not get again.

"Okay," she said. "I'll do it."

"Which? Which?"

She spoke as carelessly as she could for a suddenly dry mouth and a thudding heart.

"Gimmel," she said. "The bridge."

T W E L V E

The Bridge

Lesley had nerved herself to get on with it at once, but first there was food. They sat around the fire and toasted bits of hard, garlicky sausage, slices of bread, and tomatoes (most of which fell off the sticks into the ashes). Apart from the fact that no one was singing or talking aloud, it was so much like the riverbank wienie roasts she remembered from Saskatoon that for the first time in ages she felt a bit homesick. Then she realized that the pain in her chest wasn't homesickness, and that the only reason she was wishing to be somewhere else was because it would be safer.

"Why *dafka* you choose *gimmel*?" whispered Shula in her ear. "I think better you choose other."

117

"Why?"

Shula munched a bite out of her burnt-sausage sandwich and then said, "Why the four winds you think?"

"Have you done it?"

"Me? Don't make jokes."

"Who has done it, then?"

Shula looked around the circle of firelit faces. "Noami. David. Ofer."

"And?"

Shula shrugged and looked glum.

"No one else? No one?"

"You can change if you want."

Lesley didn't answer. The hot tomato in her sandwich burned her mouth, and she threw it angrily into the fire.

David stood up and wiped his hands on the sides of his jeans. Then he came over and crouched by her.

"You ready? We must to be in *kitta* not too late." For some reason he spoke to her in English, which was a great effort for him. This scared her more than anything, somehow.

"Yuh. Okay," said Lesley gruffly.

David beckoned to Ofer and he came over.

"Ofer go with you, show the bridge. He don't stay. You do alone, okay?" He fumbled in his pocket and handed her a long piece of white chalk. "Put in *kees.*" He indicated the pocket of her shirt.

Lesley stood up and Shula stood up, too. Shula stuffed a couple of salt-cracker bagels into her pocket. "For after," she whispered, and gave Lesley's arm a mighty squeeze of encouragement. Ofer beckoned. All the others were silent, watching. Lesley found her feet wouldn't move.

118

"H-how long will it take?" she asked, trying to sound offhand.

"You quick, nothing go bad, half hour."

Nothing go bad? What could go bad?

There was nothing else for it. Lesley told her feet to move, and they moved, following Ofer into the dark scrub forest.

Ofer didn't talk as they made their way through the darkness. He had a flashlight, but he wasn't using it. It seemed a long way. Her thoughts began to terrify her and it seemed better to try to chat.

"Is there always a test for joining the Movement?"

"Not like this. Not for us."

"What then?"

"When we joined," he said in Hebrew, "we were eleven, little kids. We were in a very exciting movie, and our *madrikh* called us out, and the test was to go at once without grumbling. But we expected it. . . ."

"So why do I have a test?"

"Well . . . you're new. You're from abroad. Besides—" He froze, clutching her arm. *"Sheket!"* he breathed.

She stayed still and silent. Now she could hear an engine, and soon they saw the headlights above them, throwing shadows as it rounded a bend and growled by on their road.

"Army jeep," whispered Ofer. "Patrol. Come on."

"What were you going to say before—about me?"

"I don't remember."

"Yes you do. You said 'besides.' Besides, I wasn't very nice at first and nobody—nobody liked me."

He threw her a swift, startled look. "I wasn't going to say that. Look—there's the bridge."

Lesley had forgotten to be afraid. Ofer was hardly older than herself, but he was confident, and he was, after all, a boy. He knew the ropes. She felt safe with him. But now she followed his pointing finger, and saw stretched across the glinting dark river a great black, solid shadow.

She could make out some kind of broken shape that must once have been a handrail, and below, a tangle of struts causing faint ripples where they entered the water. It looked very, very rickety.

Her whole body turned cold and she found herself clutching Ofer's hand.

"Don't you want to?" he whispered kindly.

She shook her head, though whether to say no, she'd rather do anything else in the world, or whether to say he was wrong, wasn't clear to either of them. But she knew that, anyway, she was going to do it, though why she must she didn't understand. No one was pushing her, other than herself.

Ofer bent his head to her ear.

"Listen. Leave your shoes next to one leg of the bridge, so you can be sure to find them. Walk into the river a little way. Find a place where you can climb. Be careful of the wood. It may be soft. On the bridge don't stand up. Okay? *Not to stand up.*" He said this in English, very strongly even though he was whispering.

"Crawl. Like this." He made motions with his arms. "In the middle there's a wide plank. Make the chalk mark on that. Big, so we see it tomorrow. Then back, into the water slowly, don't make a splash. Your shoes—and back."

She was staring at him with her mouth open. This

sounded far, far worse than she'd imagined—why hadn't they said all this to her before, about the wood being rotten, about having to crawl?

"How will I get back? Will you wait for me?"

He hesitated. "I'm not supposed to."

"So leave me the flashlight."

He looked at it in his hand. He turned to look back, the dark, dark way they had come. She willed him with all her might to break the rule and wait for her. She prayed for it.

He said, "Okay. I wait. Now go. *Kol tuv.*"

She turned and started down the bank toward the river and the bridge.

The last rainfall had been the day before—a late shower—and the bank was still a little slippery. Lesley clutched at the rough stems of plants as she half climbed, half slid down. Once she grabbed a thistle and it hurt so much she nearly cried out. Then she was beside the water.

At once she felt better. Being near a river always made her feel strong and positive. She took a deep breath, and the muddy smell filled her lungs.

The bridge loomed above her. It was not really very big. In its days of use, it couldn't have carried anything wider than a cart, if that. Now it was lopsided and neglected, as if it would soon fall into the river.

She could see the tangle of barbed wire across the ends of the bridge on both sides. Reaching its deeper shadow, she felt still safer. No one could see her under here. She sat down on the damp bank to take off her shoes and socks.

It was while she was carefully rolling up the legs of her

jeans that she heard a sound that made her head snap up and her hair rise on her neck.

For several seconds she sat perfectly still. Had she dreamed it? No. There it was again! An awful, eerie sound, desolate even by day, perhaps the saddest cry in nature: the forlorn braying of a donkey.

She stood up in one jump, peering with all the strength of her eye muscles into the blackness opposite. Was that something? Yes! Over there, just near the other end of the bridge at the water's edge, a vague movement, accompanied by the faintest scrunching sound—the sound of small hooves crushing wet stems.

Without a moment's further hesitation, she waded into the water. It was colder than she'd expected, and she gasped as the ripples crept up her legs. The first struts seemed far away, and the water was near the ridge of her rolled-up jeans by the time she reached them. The donkey on the other side uttered little grunting sounds as if calling her. She began to climb.

Her eyes, completely adjusted to the darkness, picked out the joins in the bridge supports quite easily, and her bare feet seemed to have eyes of their own as they found steps. Almost at once her right hand was groping along the overhanging top surface for some upright grip to pull herself up by.

She grasped a post, tested it, felt it sway in its socket. She felt a pang of fear. If she made it take her weight and it broke, she would go straight into the river on her back with a splash that would bring any patrol within miles down on her.

She tugged at the post again. She would have to trust it, but not for long. She gave a quick heave. The post gave dangerously, but by that time she had her left elbow on the bridge, and in another moment, her stomach. Her right knee came up, gained purchase—she was up!

So far, so good! Using her elbows to pull her along, she crawled forward, commando fashion. The bridge was horribly unsteady. The wooden planks felt soggy and rotten under her hands. The boards cracked and creaked and the whole bridge swayed on its piles. Through the warped slats, she could see the Jordan sliding past underneath her.

The donkey brayed again, a double heehaw, heehaw.

"Sshhh—shhh," she breathed between clenched teeth.

Now she was in the middle. Here was a good wide plank to make the mark on. She reached under herself, found the pocket of her shirt, and stuck her fingers in, searching for the chalk.

It was gone.

It couldn't be! She rolled on her back and fumbled from one pocket corner to the other. No chalk. It must have dropped out! All she could find was the couple of salt-stick bagels Shula had slipped in her pocket "for after."

Well! Did it matter? Ofer, back there, could see her. He could report that she'd made it.

But it wouldn't be the same as standing up there tomorrow in daylight and seeing her mark, the proof she'd "passed."

If only she could get a couple of sticks and lay them in an X . . . But where?

The donkey brayed again. An answer!

Obvious. She began to crawl forward.

She could see the donkey now, standing by the foot of the bridge. He was looking at her. Could it possibly be Eeyore? So far from home? She was almost up to the rolls of barbed wire. Lesley slid feet first, backward, over the edge of the bridge. The rail was stronger here, and it was easy to lower herself into the water. She waded slowly and carefully ashore.

The donkey stretched his nose out toward her, like a dog smelling at a stranger. She put forward her hand and touched him. He felt like warm velvet, and his breath was lovely on her wet, cold hand. Warmth, companionship, a fellow creature alive in this cold, scary darkness! She stumbled to the bank and put both arms around his soft shaggy neck, burying her face in his mane.

"Eeyore! Is it really you?" she whispered.

She ran her hand down the inside of his foreleg. Yes, there was the hobble rope, knotted around his fetlock, ragged in the middle where it had broken, and here the other frayed end joined to the other leg.

"Bad boy, you've run away!"

She took a bagel out of her pocket and felt his soft lips tickling her palm as he gently accepted it, then listened to the deep, satisfied scrunch as he bit it up. She rubbed him under his jaw, and he put his big hard head against her comfortingly.

She held one of his long ears and whispered to him, "I wish I could take you back with me! Then that rotten Mustapha would never beat you again!"

Just at that moment she heard a soft, low, frantically urgent whistle. She nearly jumped out of her skin.

Turning, she saw Ofer's dim outline on the far bank. He was waving his arms at her, making great beckoning gestures.

She realized, suddenly, where she was.

She was in Jordan. Enemy territory!

The thought of it was like a bolt of electricity passing straight through her. What had she done? What had possessed her? Instantly she turned and started to wade back into the river. Then she stopped.

Eeyore was following her!

She felt his nose butting softly into her back. She heard the splash as his forefeet struck the water close behind her.

She turned to him. He had a crude halter rope around his neck, which she caught hold of, and tried to turn his head and urge him to go back. She pushed his head with all her might. It was like pushing a furry rock.

Feeling a turbulent mixture of desperation and anxiety, she turned away from him and, far less cautiously than before, began to plow through the deepening water to the first supports.

Eeyore splashed after her with no caution at all.

Now she was really frightened. He sounded as loud as Niagara Falls. Surely anyone within miles could hear! Was this her fault? Had she *enticed* him to follow her?

As she climbed like a scared monkey up the struts and hauled herself frantically onto the bridge, she could hear him making all sorts of commotion below and wished he would drop dead.

Instead he stood belly-deep in the stream till he saw her descend again on the other side. Then he plunged into the central channel of the river and began to swim.

He only had to swim a few strokes. Almost at once he found his footing again, and before Lesley had stumbled ashore on her own side, the donkey had caught up with her and was pushing his dripping chin up against her shoulder.

Ofer grabbed her the second she was within his reach and shook her like a cotton duster.

"*Tembelit!* Idiot! What the four winds did you think you were doing?" He sounded absolutely furious and frantic. She thought he was going to slap her around the head.

Her teeth were chattering and she was trembling all over. She couldn't say a word, only weakly tried to push Ofer's rough hands away and get her breath. The moment he released her, she sank to the ground.

Eeyore nudged her sympathetically.

"Get out of here, you stupid ugly brute!" hissed Ofer, frenziedly trying to shove him back into the river. "Get back where you belong!" Eeyore stood there, unmoving and unmovable, his muzzle resting on the top of Lesley's head.

Ofer dragged Lesley roughly to her feet. "Come on! Hurry! Leave him behind!"

They began stumbling up the bank together, Ofer holding tightly to Lesley's arm. Lesley's feet were so numb with cold that she completely failed to notice that she had left her shoes behind. She didn't even feel the stones underfoot as they scrambled back to the path. Ofer recklessly shone his flashlight so that they could get back to the others quicker.

Their frightened blood pounded in their ears so hard that they probably wouldn't have heard the gunshot that

Ofer, at least, was fully expecting, even if it had gone off right behind them. So they certainly didn't hear the delicate patter of the donkey's little hooves as he came trotting placidly along in their wake.

THIRTEEN

The Gray Ghost

It seemed a hundred years before Ofer's wavering torchlight coincided with the glowing embers of the campfire, and flicked around the huddled figures and frightened faces of the others.

As the two of them burst into the little clearing, the whole group rose as one and flung themselves forward as if to envelop them and protect them. At least, that was how it seemed to Lesley. As she felt their warm bodies close to her, and Shula's comfortable fat person clutching her free arm, she had a startling sense of oneness with them. Her fear, half-paralyzing a moment before, dwindled almost to nothing.

Now they were all together, with her in their midst as one of them, an outsider no longer, it suddenly seemed to her that nothing bad could ever happen.

The questions were coming thick and fast.

"Where were you?"

"Why were you so long?"

"Someone saw you?"

"What happened?"

And from observant, practical Shula, a subdued wail: "Where the four winds are your *shoes*?"

There was a sudden silence. Everyone looked downward while Ofer played his flashlight on her bare, filthy feet.

"I left them there," she whispered through dry lips. "At the—at the bridge."

The whispered cacophony burst out again.

"Why? Are you crazy? What *happened*—tell us!"

Aviva's voice topped the rest. "Let's get back. We can talk safer at home."

The boys tramped down the last glows and smothered them with earth. Others hastily gathered up all the remains of the food, the rugs and sacks, and Ofer went ahead with the flashlight as the straggling procession started back toward the kibbutz.

Esther came to Lesley.

"Do you want my shoes?"

"No thanks."

"Your teeth are chattering. Here, you'd better take them."

She made Lesley put them on. One of the boys threw a

blanket over her shoulders and she gratefully wrapped it around herself. Suddenly Danny—clever Danny—stopped.

"Someone must go back and get her shoes."

There was a shrinking silence.

"What's wrong with picking them up in the morning?"

"If anyone found them first . . . They're marked."

All items of clothing were indelibly inked with their owners' names.

"I'll go," said David when no one else spoke.

"No," said Naomi. "I'll go."

Before anyone could stop her, she had grabbed the flashlight from Ofer and gone haring off into the dark. The boys looked at each other with faint masculine unease. But girls and boys were supposed to be equal. . . . They let her go, and the procession started forward again.

Suddenly they were all electrified by a scream.

It was echoed irrepressibly by several girls in the group. Shula squealed like a piglet being picked up by its tail, and hid her face in her hands.

Several of the boys turned and started back at a run. One of them, a clumsy good-natured boy called Amnon, tripped and fell. All was confusion, almost panic. Lesley found both Esther and Shula desperately clinging to her. They were all looking back into the darkness toward the river.

A little figure came flying out of the scrub and ran headlong into David and Ofer. It was Naomi, gibbering with the first real fear she'd ever felt.

"A thing! A ghost! A thing!" she gasped. "God save me! I bumped into a great, gray, ghosty—thing!"

It was the first mention of God Lesley ever remembered hearing in the kibbutz, and suddenly she began to laugh. It would have turned quickly into hysterics if Ofer hadn't seized her and shaken her again.

"*Shtok!*" he hissed fiercely. "Shut up! This is all your fault!" He turned to the others. "It's a cursed donkey she brought back with her from the other side!"

After a moment's incredulous silence, pandemonium broke out.

Nobody could keep their voices down anymore. Some shouted questions, some burst out laughing, some just made incoherent noises. Naomi, still so white that her face was itself ghostly in the dimness, thrust it into Lesley's.

"You—brought—a donkey—" Words failed her.

"You crossed the *river?*" David asked, his voice rising to a bleat.

"Right to the other side?"

"She's mad! Mad completely!"

"You could have been shot!"

"Or taken prisoner!"

"All the ground over there's probably mined!"

Lesley had never dreamed of such a thing. She felt icy waves of too-late terror washing over her. "B-but," she stammered, "Eeyore was standing on the only ground I stood on!"

"*Who?*"

"Eeyore," she said faintly. "There."

They all turned again, and sure enough, reaching out his nose to explore David's neck, was the great gray Thing himself.

David leaped away with a yell. Shula broke down into

shrill, whinnying giggles. *"Ma pitom?* What next?" she kept saying hysterically.

Aviva once again took charge.

"Leave it. We're going!"

"But it'll follow us!" Ofer said despairingly. "It followed her right across the river. It had to swim. Do you think it won't walk half a kilometer? The thing's in love with her or something. . . . She's put a spell on it!"

"I haven't! I haven't!" Lesley cried. "All I did was give it a bagel—"

That was all it needed. The tide of hysteria rose. Several people, Shula among them, simply gave way and sank to the ground, rolling about with uncontrollable laughter.

"She went to Jordan—"

"And stood there in a minefield—"

"Feeding some flea-bitten Arab donkey—"

"With *our bagels!*"

Even Ofer seemed to lose some of his anger. As for Amnon, the tears were running down his plump cheeks and he was giving great cowlike moans. People were holding each other up, laughing helplessly. They weren't able to take a grip on themselves, and it took a sudden stern grown-up voice from above to shock them back into their scattered wits.

"What's going on there?"

They froze, each holding his position like children playing statues. The shout had to be repeated before David found his voice.

"It's only us—we're from Kfar Orde—having a *p-p-p'oola!*"

"You're making a lot of noise about it," the soldier's voice retorted. "And it's late. Go home. Now!"

They needed no second telling. In a frantic scuffle they gathered themselves and their possessions together once more and scrambled in scared silence back onto the road. They could see the outline of the soldier standing, hands on hips, with his Sten gun hooked carelessly in the bend of his arm, watching them.

In every mind was a single thought: What if the donkey emerged on the road after them? Lesley willed him with all her mind to stay under cover. Maybe what Ofer had said about a spell was true, because he did.

They arrived back at their *kitta* by a special route that avoided the busiest parts of the kibbutz. Adda, their housemother, didn't sleep in the *kitta,* and the night watch didn't start checking up that they were all in bed until around eleven-thirty. Incredible as it seemed, it was still only ten of when the last of them got safely inside. Esther did a quick head count to make sure.

With unspoken accord, they all squeezed into Lesley's bedroom. Lesley climbed straight under the covers fully dressed, and Shula piled more bedclothes over her icy legs.

"You'll make your sheets filthy," Aviva said.

"I don't care. I'm so cold!"

"Have a hot shower."

Lesley didn't reply. She was trembling too much.

"Now then," said Danny, his blue eyes bright and stern, "tell us what happened."

It all came out in a confused jumble, with Ofer chipping

in and Shula translating the bits Lesley couldn't manage in her still-basic Hebrew. Ofer's version didn't agree with Lesley's completely. His tone was bewildered, almost accusing.

"I couldn't believe it—she got to the middle, and then she just kept going—"

"I wanted sticks, to make a mark—the chalk had fallen out—"

"As if that mattered—"

"And the donkey—it was sort of calling. . . ."

"Calling? What are you talking about?" they all asked incredulously. She couldn't explain. Kibbutz children hadn't much feeling for animals. How could she say that Eeyore was like a person to her, a friend that she'd helplessly watched being ill treated, and there he was and she wanted to—to meet him, talk to him. . . .

She looked around at their faces and knew that not in a million years could she explain that. It seemed, now, idiotic, even to her. She didn't blame Ofer and the others if they were angry with her. She'd taken an absolutely mad, unacceptable risk. It was beyond daring, incredible in its stupidity. Any one of them, even the bravest, the biggest show-off, would as soon have jumped out of an airplane without a parachute as do what she'd done.

And for what? A pair of sticks, misplaced pride—and a "cursed donkey."

They all fell silent. One or two of them shook their heads in total bewilderment, or made the "tra-la-la" gesture—one finger corkscrewing at the temple—and one by one they padded away to their own rooms until only her three roommates were left.

134

Ofer, who had been standing over her bed, hands on hips, now looked at her silently for another moment, heaved a tremendous sigh of incomprehension, and turned to get undressed. The three girls automatically turned their faces away. Lesley lay facing the wall, still numb with the aftereffects of strong feelings. Aviva went off to have a shower. But Shula sat on Lesley's bed, her hands still slowly, thoughtfully, rubbing Lesley's cold legs through the bedclothes.

"What about your shoes?"

"I'll go and get them early tomorrow morning," said Lesley in a flat voice.

"And—the donkey?"

She didn't answer. She swallowed hard. A great hard lump had come into her throat. She reached up and switched off her light.

"You sleep in your *begadim*?" asked Shula.

Lesley turned her face into the pillow. She knew she was going to have to cry, long and hard, before all the tension built up inside her was released. Shula understood. With a sigh like Ofer's, she stood up, to leave her as much alone as was possible.

"You are funny old nut case," she said sadly. "Crazy completely. But I like you. Maybe I crazy, too."

F O U R T E E N

Face to Face

Lesley slept badly and woke early, uncomfortable in her dirty, clumsy clothes. She looked
at her watch. It was just on five-thirty, and
dawn would soon lighten the eastern sky.
Adda didn't come to wake them till after six-
thirty. She would just have time.

She got up quietly and hurried to the
shower room. A hot shower made her feel a
lot better. She watched the water washing
down her legs, carrying the telltale river mud
away. She crept back to the room, threw her
dirty clothes in the laundry basket, and put on
clean ones. Then she got out her key and
opened her box. Inside was the half bar of
chocolate each person got on Friday morn-

ings, which she'd saved. She wasn't hungry now, but she would be.

She glanced at her diary and her writing pad. If she couldn't explain her actions to herself in her head, how was she going to write it down? In her diary—or to Noah?

She put on a sweater and rubber boots and hurried out into the pale morning. The light was pearly gray. The grass looked milky from the myriad drops of condensation on the spiderwebs, and the palm trees shook their tousled giants' heads gently against the lightening sky.

The kibbutz main gates were already open to let the field workers out. Lesley slipped out unseen. In a few minutes she was cutting wet swaths through the dew-soaked brush on the way to the river. A patrol went by in a jeep but didn't bother with her. When it was out of sight, she sprinted the rest of the way across the flat, open part and stood for a moment on the top of the bank.

She couldn't see the bridge from here. It was hidden in one of the twists and folds of the terrain. Straight ahead of her lay the orange grove of Mustapha's father, and beyond that, their village, not golden now but still in shadow. It was hard to pick it out. Arab buildings at any time of day were like a natural part of the landscape. . . . Beyond were the hills, not pink and speckled now because the sun was just rising behind them, but still dark and rather sinister in their naked stillness.

Enemy territory . . . and she had been there.

She started down the riverbank, following their tracks from the night before, till she came to the clearing where they had picnicked. There she stopped cold.

She hadn't precisely forgotten about Eeyore. She'd dreamed about him—tangled, garbled dreams—most of the night. But since he hadn't followed the group, she supposed he'd gone home. She simply couldn't think about how complicated it would be if he hadn't.

So when she suddenly came upon him, nosing among the last bits of food they had left lying about, she felt her heart jerk into her throat.

Eeyore lifted his head, ghostly in the gray dawn. His long, dew-wet ears were pricked; his jaws slid from side to side as he chewed a crust of bread. His breath showed in a little cloud. His great dark eyes dwelled softly on Lesley.

She stretched out her hand, and he moved like a shadow toward her and dropped his velvet nose into her hand.

"You nuisance!" she whispered. And then, in Hebrew, *"Khamor katan sheli*—my little donkey." She took his wet ear in her hand and kissed it. He butted her gently in the stomach with his nose.

She felt in her jeans pocket for the chocolate she had brought for herself. She fed a piece to him joyfully—he seemed astonished by the strange, delicious taste and tossed his head up and down.

Remembering Ofer's words, she made magic passes at him. "You're under a spell. You can't move! Wait here," she said, and set off for the bridge.

Spell or no spell, he followed at her shoulder.

They walked through the scrub together. It seemed so ordinary and unalarming in the growing daylight. And so short! There was the bridge already—and there, thank heaven, were her shoes.

She ran to fetch them. Tucking the socks deep into the toes, she tied the laces together and slung them over one shoulder. She was just starting back when a movement across the river caught her eye and fixed her to the spot.

It was Mustapha.

He rose up out of the long grass and reeds on the other shore and stood looking at her out of his expressionless, coal-black eyes, one hand on the base of the bridge.

If the donkey had looked ghostly, how much more so did this strange figure, who, wet as he was, with his color-less shirt and black hair plastered to his skin, appeared like some river djinn, risen in eerie silence from the water itself.

They stood staring at each other, divided only by the narrow river. Lesley had a feeling they must stand there forever, for how could the first move be made, and by whom? But it was she who made it at last. She raised her hand level with her shoulder in greeting—the same sort of half-wave that she had given once or twice from the culture house balcony.

But he didn't answer her greeting. In a rough, low voice, he spoke to her across the border between their countries.

"My donkey," he said in Arabic.

Ah, her hard work with Akhmed! Now it paid off. In a flash the right words came to her. "Not yours," she said, pointing to him. "Mine."

"You thief," came his clear reply.

"He choose me," she said.

"My donkey," the boy repeated fiercely. "Send him back."

"You come get him."

139

He hesitated. She saw him look at the water, and an irrepressible shiver passed over his thin body. He looked so wet already that she guessed he must have been crouching in the grass for much of the night—trying to pluck up courage to come across, perhaps.

Now he glanced upward, toward the top of the bank on her side, where the road was—where the soldiers were.

He took a breath, made up his mind, and stepped into the water. But something stopped him like a glass wall.

He frowned, angry with himself, his black brows knitted together. He looked at her helplessly and shook his head. She saw he couldn't do it. He was simply not able.

Lesley stood irresolute. Of course, he was right. Eeyore was his. No, he belonged to his father. Not a nice man . . . She had watched him hit Mustapha over trifles, as the boy hit the beast. What might he do to him for losing the donkey that was vital to their livelihood? What might he have done already?

In her Arabic class, Lesley had asked Akhmed for words, words she needed for her imagined conversations with Mustapha. Puzzled, he'd supplied them and she had learned them. Now she was able to ask, "Your father beat you?"

For answer he turned his shoulder and showed her the black stripes on his shirt.

Lesley's heart shriveled with pity. For another moment they looked at each other. Soon the sun would be up beyond those round hills that loomed over Mustapha's little gray figure—proudly erect, tense with defiance, yet with a desperate, wordless appeal on his exhausted face.

"You not beat the donkey anymore."

He frowned and cocked his head as if he hadn't heard, but she knew she had it right and that he understood.

She raised her voice and put command into it.

"You will not beat him!"

His eyes darted hungrily toward the donkey. He shrugged his shoulders.

"No," she said. "Promise." She held up her hand again, stiffly this time, in the traditional—in the West—gesture for taking an oath.

He didn't move, only scowled.

She didn't know what to do. It was getting lighter and lighter. If any adult on either side of the river should happen to see them . . . ! Yet she couldn't—she *could not* return Eeyore into Mustapha's untender hands without being *sure*.

"Do you believe in God?" she asked him desperately.

He looked still more blank. And now suddenly the sun's first rays seemed to burst over the rim of the eastern hills. The sky was pale blue and the air was loud with bird and insect noises. The world was waking up. They couldn't hope for secrecy for more than a very few minutes longer.

The boy's face contracted into a grimace of urgency.

"Quick!" he called. "Send him!"

"Do you believe in—in Allah?" Lesley persisted.

"I believe! Send him!"

"Promise in Allah's name you don't beat him!"

Now he understood fully. His eyes narrowed. She could see he was amazed and bewildered. What could it matter to her?

141

"Without beating he won't go," he said.

"Not true. Look!"

Lesley turned and put her hand out to Eeyore, who had wandered some yards away to browse. She clicked her tongue to call him. He flung up his head and trotted to her. She patted him and kissed his nose. She took out the chocolate, broke another square off, and gave it to him.

"What you give him?" Mustapha called in a low voice.

"Chocolate."

"Chocolate!"

"But he likes lots of things. Carrots. Apples. Sugar."

The boy gazed at her unbelievingly. In his look she read: "Waste on an animal what we don't have for ourselves!" For the first time in her life, Lesley got an inkling of the nature of real poverty and felt suddenly ashamed.

"Look!" she said. She petted Eeyore, rubbed him under the jaw, and hugged his head. "Love him. That doesn't cost money."

The boy watched, shook his head, then grinned. "Okay," he said unexpectedly in English.

And now Lesley had to find the way. There was only one.

The sun was up. She had to do it now. She glanced around. At the same time, Mustapha did the same. They were quite alone. . . . As if by a signal, they both stepped into the water from opposite banks.

Lesley held Eeyore by the halter. The river crept up his legs, up her boots. Mustapha waded toward her. When the water was up to his knees and was slopping into her boots, they stopped with a few yards between them.

Eeyore stopped, too. He would go no farther unless she did.

She took the remains of the chocolate out of her pocket. "Catch!" she said to the boy, and threw it.

His hands flew up, and the chocolate landed between them. He opened his hands slowly and stared into them, as if at some wonder that lay there. Then he held the slab out to the donkey and clicked his tongue.

At the same moment Lesley let go of the halter, stepped back in the river, and gave his haunches a hard shove with both hands.

Eeyore smelled the chocolate and stretched his neck. Lesley shoved him again. He lunged forward, swam a few strokes through the deeper water, and in another moment Mustapha had caught hold of his halter and was pulling him back to the opposite shore.

Lesley stood in the river and watched. She had a fear that Mustapha could not give any of the chocolate to Eeyore. If that happened, she would know that she had delivered him back into the hands of a heartless master.

But Mustapha surprised her. As soon as he and Eeyore were back on dry land, he peeled the paper off the chocolate, broke it into two equal pieces, and held them up for Lesley to see. Then he gave one to the donkey, and the other, with a great grin of gleeful relish, he stuffed into his own mouth.

She smiled broadly. But her smile faded. The boy was eating the chocolate with closed eyes and a look of bliss on his face so strong it was almost violent. Then it was finished, and he grinned all over his face, looking younger than the youngest kibbutz child in his relief and happiness. He caught hold of Eeyore's neck and leaped on his back. Then he glanced back at Lesley.

"Thanks," he called softly.

"Go. *Salaam.*"

"*Salaam*—Leslee!"

Boy and donkey began trotting along the edge of the water, upriver toward the village. Lesley jogged along on her side, keeping level.

"How you know my name?"

He grinned again, reached into his shirt, and pulled something out of his belt. He waved it at her.

It was filthy and wet, but she could see—or guess—what it was. Her photo. And, yes, now she remembered, her name and the date had been written on the back by her orderly mother.

"What's your name?" she called jerkily as she ran.

And back across the water, faintly now, for he was ahead of her, came back the astonishing reply: "Mustapha!"

She stopped running.

Of course, thousands of Arabs were called Mustapha. But still!

Lesley rubbed her eyes, panting. The sun was shining into them and striking sparks off the water and off the drops of moisture everywhere. When she looked again, they were gone, boy and donkey—two gray little ghosts vanished with the coming of sunlight.

144

Crisis

When Lesley came back to the *kitta* that morning, still with a sense of magic upon her after this strange encounter, she was brought speedily down to earth.

Adda was waiting for her, her arms full of dirty sheets.

"How is it possible to get sheets so filthy?" Lesley hung her head.

"You got so dirty and then went to bed without showering? Lesley, I'm shocked at you! In all my years as a *metapelet*, I've never seen anything like it!" She often said this about the latest "outrage."

"Sorry, Adda. I was so tired."

"I hope you're clean now at least!"

145

Lesley nodded. Adda was fussy about cleanliness—so fussy that Lesley hoped she wouldn't think to ask where she had been so early. And she didn't. She went away tutting over the sheets, and Lesley slipped back into the room where the others were getting ready for breakfast.

Ofer swung around as she entered. "Oh! I see you got them all right," he said with relief, looking at her shoes.

Shula said, "How you feel?"

"Okay," said Lesley. "Fine."

Nobody else said anything. They had breakfast in a subdued mood, and passed the day with eyes averted even from each other. Suspense gripped them all. Would the soldier who had seen them report them? Would there be any other kind of comeback?

After school, during which she had hardly been able to concentrate, Lesley went to visit her mother in the kitchens. Never could she have dreamed of telling her about her adventure, but she needed to see her and be near her just the same.

But she wasn't there.

"Where's *ima*?" she shouted above the racket of dishwashing for three hundred lunch-eaters.

"Miriam's not working here anymore, *motik*. She asked to be moved to the *communa*."

The *communa* was where all the kibbutz members' clothes were taken care of—washed, pressed, and mended. It was a light, airy building with different rooms for the different jobs. Lesley found her mother seated before a strange machine, like a huge roller, which ironed trousers and sheets.

"Hi, Mom," Lesley said. "What are you doing in here?"

146

Miriam Shelby looked up. "Hallo, hon. It's my first day. How'm I doin'?" She showed Lesley how she worked the machine with foot pedals.

"Great. But why did you want to change? I thought you liked working in the kitchen."

"I never said that."

"Well, didn't you?"

"No," she said grimly. "I hated it."

"I don't blame you! But you stuck it so long!"

"One doesn't like to be a nuisance." She thrust a folded sheet into the roller and made it take it in. Steam rose. "But I was. All the time I worked there, I was a—what's that word for a nagger?"

"*Nudnik.* But I don't believe it—you? How were you a *nudnik?*"

Her mother sighed and took her foot off the pedal.

"I couldn't believe it at first. When I saw they didn't even try to keep kosher."

"Well, but, Mom, it's different here."

"So your father says. He agrees with it! Can you believe that? He says we don't need all that here—all the laws that kept us Jewish all down the centuries, now we've got our own country we can just throw them out the window! And there was I, working in the kitchen, feeding hundreds of people with heaven knows what, no separate *milchiker* and *fleishiker* dishes, nothing! You know that stuff they call *spek*? You know what that is? —I hope you never eat that, by the way!"

"Why, what is it?" Lesley asked uneasily, having just had some for breakfast.

"It's fat bacon, that's what. Can you imagine that? A

Jewish community, eating pork? I heard they used to *raise pigs* here, till the rabbis stopped it!" She was talking quietly, but her voice was full of passion.

Lesley had heard about it, what a good way it had been of using up all the wasted food, what a good price they got from the Christian Arabs for the meat, and how indignant the kibbutzniks were when the rabbis made them stop.

But she didn't say anything. She just put her arm around her mother and said, "I guess it was tough for you."

"I felt in shock the whole time. And I couldn't keep quiet—I think I've been driving them mad in there. In the end I asked to be transferred. They're nice women, but there were no tears when I left!"

"But they like you. Your birthday . . ."

"I said they were nice." She sighed deeply, and suddenly, astonishingly, she burst out, "It's not so easy, being married, Lesley."

"You think it's all Dad's fault?"

"Do you think this whole business was my idea?"

Lesley stared at her mother. She had scarcely ever heard a word of criticism of her father from her in her life.

"Don't you love Dad?" she asked in a shocked voice.

Her mother looked her straight in the face. She had a look Lesley hadn't seen before—a direct, unguarded look.

"Love the stubborn old . . . ? I adore the ground he walks on! But *oooh,* how I could beat him about the head sometimes, honest to God I could!"

And she shoved another sheet into the presser and sent up a fierce cloud of steam.

• • •

148

A stubborn old . . . ? Her father, *a stubborn old . . . ?* Lesley
left the *communa* and hurried straight to the cowsheds. She
had to have a look at him, this "stubborn old . . ." of a
father. A look with new eyes!

He was shut in the crude shower that was attached to the
refet. Men who did dirty or smelly work usually showered
before they came home. She could hear the rushing water.
She knocked on the door.

"That you, Dad?"

"Yeah, Les. Hi. Whaddaya want?"

"Nothing. I came to visit you."

"Gee, thanks! Thought you'd never get around to it!"

The water went off and after a moment he put his wet
head around the door. "Sure that's all? Maybe you'd like to
watch me sweat a bit? Too bad, I'm through for the day."

He closed the door again.

"Dad," she called.

"Nu?"

"D'you like working in the *refet?*"

There was a pause. She could hear him drying himself.

"Nearly killed me at first—now it can be told."

"Why? Too hard?"

"That, and other things. I'm getting used to it. Did I tell
you they're sending me on a course?"

"What kind?"

"Learn to be a better cowboy, I guess. There's more to
dairy management than you might think."

"Is that what you want?"

"Nobody asked me," he said, but humorously, not as if
he minded.

149

"Did you hear Mom's changed jobs?"

"Yes. Good thing. She wasn't happy."

"I didn't know."

"I did."

The door opened and he came out, buttoning his clean flannel shirt, with his curly hair slicked back. He looked very fit. All the flab was gone.

"Nu, Princess, give the old cowpoke a kiss."

"Who're you calling Princess?" she asked.

"In the nicest way. You're my princess and I'm proud of you."

She kissed him. His old smell—quality after-shave, hair tonic, tobacco—was gone. Now she could smell carbolic soap, and cows, and good health.

He returned her inspection. "You're lookin' real good these days. Both my gals are. I go for the natural look." He took her face in his hands. "Are you happy here, Les?" he asked, suddenly serious.

"I think so."

"Beginning to feel part of it?"

The bridge flashed through Lesley's head.

"Yes."

"Good. You're going to need to before we're much older."

"What do you mean?"

"The situation. That's what I mean. It's bad and going to get worse. I wouldn't be surprised if we're in for a war."

Meir, their teacher, talked about the "situation," but calmly, trying not to alarm them. Baruch, the class pessimist and politician, didn't bother.

150

"The Egyptians are out to get us," he had declared, only yesterday. "We shamed them in '48, we shamed them again in '56. When you shame Arabs, they never forget. The Jordanians, too. And the Syrians. And the—"

Her father was still holding her face. She suddenly said, "I suppose wars are what *menschen* like."

He dropped his hands and looked at her with a sort of horrified amazement.

"What are you getting at, Les? Do you think I brought you here to test my manhood by putting you and your mother into danger?"

"I don't know, Dad. Did you?"

He stared at her for a long moment. Then he said abruptly, "It's teatime. Let's go."

He turned on his heel. She followed him out of the cowshed into the afternoon sunshine.

The bridge business was never mentioned again. Lesley and the other kids knew they had tweaked the very beard of mortal danger, and gotten clean away with it. It scared them to think about it. But the odd truth was, they didn't think about it very much, because now the "situation" loomed far larger, far more alarming, and it pushed their private adventure right into the background.

Lesley had never been especially interested in "news," but now she fell victim to an Israeli habit, strongest, of course, in times of crisis: news fever.

Every hour on the hour, radios went on all over the kibbutz. You could hear them, far and near, from house windows, from transistors people carried about with them, even at meals in the dining hall. In the *kitta* there was only one radio, and the kids wanted to listen to every news bulletin like everyone else, but the teachers refused to cooperate, especially the English teacher.

"Not during *my* lessons," she said firmly. "This mania for listening to the news all the time just exaggerates everyone's fears. Once a day is plenty."

"Once a day!" objected Baruch. "How can we know what's happening? There's a new development every five minutes!"

"Rubbish, Baruch. You're obsessed. So President Nasser has ordered the United Nations peace-keeping force to withdraw from Egypt." Always ready to make a lesson out of everything, she wrote this sentence on the board in English. "Withdraw, to pull out. Write it. And did they go?"

"YES!" chorused the class. "They—have—gone!" added Esther. "Just. Present perfect, right?"

"Present not at all perfect," said Danny, earning a rueful laugh from the others. *"Akhshav sh'hem—"*

"English, Danny, please—"

"Now they have gone, is all clean for Egyptians to send their army into Sinai."

"All *clear*. Right. But we don't know if they will, so—"

"They will! They will send. Future *tense,*" said Danny cleverly.

And so it was. The whole country was gearing for action—for a war of survival.

The first real sign in the kibbutz was the rapid disappearance of more and more of the men. Many of the unmarried younger women were called up, too.

Sometimes Lesley would see people going off in the daytime, singly or in groups as their army numbers were announced on the radio or as khaki-painted trucks and jeeps arrived to collect them. She'd wake up in the morning to find one or more of the kids in the group with long faces because an older brother, or father, or uncle had gone in the night.

Boaz, their youth leader; Shula's father and her brother Rami (of the binoculars); Ofer's brother, Adam, and his sister's husband, Brosh, whose job was to tell the kids where to work and who, in his leisure time, was a star of the football team—gone. The army even took Moshe the gardener—old as he seemed to them, he was an officer in the reserves and went early. Ayala took over the *noi*. She was much less strict then Moshe, but Shula and Lesley missed him. They felt they had to work as hard as he would expect, even without him there to supervise and scold.

One morning they got to class to find no Meir.

They were deeply dismayed. They'd had Meir as their class teacher since they'd started school. He was their best adult friend. Till then he'd been sort of holding their hands about the crisis, taking the best view without hiding anything, keeping them informed, but reassured. Now he'd gone. They felt abandoned.

The English teacher took over their other lessons. She was unbending, rather evasive about the crisis, and not as good as Meir at anything.

As things began to look worse and worse—the Egyptians

really had moved their forces right up into the Sinai, against the southern border with Israel, and war now seemed to be inevitable—the anti-Arab feeling began to spread. It came out of fear, because the Arab radio stations were broadcasting terrible threats.

Akhmed kept coming twice a week for their Arabic lessons, but nobody wanted to learn. Even Lesley, his star pupil, didn't. She was affected by the general feeling. Eventually, one day in the middle of May—a day of *hamsin,* the hot desert wind that blew fifty days of the year and could drive people a little crazy—Gadi, who was getting very macho and aggressive, just got up and walked out of the class because Akhmed asked him politely to take his feet off the desk.

Akhmed hesitated, then excused himself and went after him.

The class sat in silence, listening. After a moment they heard Gadi shouting, "I don't want to learn stinking Arabic! When the war starts, you'll probably go and join Nasser, you'd like it fine if he wiped us all out!"

Shula put her hands to her ears. Everyone felt shocked. Nobody moved.

Akhmed didn't come back. Not that day and not again, ever. And there was no Meir to call them to order. The English teacher didn't say a word.

Only Adda said sadly, "I heard. To insult such a nice young man! It's against everything you've been taught. You hurt my heart, Gadi-gad." Gadi didn't speak to anyone all day. Her using his nickname, he told Yossi later, as if she loved him anyway, made him feel a complete zero.

154

They all secretly felt bad about Akhmed—but not bad enough to do anything about it.

Lesley's mother and father—her father especially—had to work harder than ever. Dairy work was mainly for men, and most of the *refet* workers had been called up, so Nat Shelby found himself doing double shifts. His course was canceled. Miriam did her stint in the laundry and then went off to help in various other branches where there was a shortage of people, doing rough work she'd never done in her life. All the women, and the younger and older people, were doing the same. Nobody grumbled.

Soon all nonessential work was abandoned. Lesley and Shula were taken out of the gardens and the lawns grew long. The group's working hours of two a day were expanded indefinitely: nobody watched the clock now. They worked wherever they were put, they worked till the job was done, and no one dreamed of shirking. They did the jobs of grown-ups. Lesley was glad she'd had time to learn how to work hard, before this crisis happened—there was no question of flinging herself onto the grass for a rest now. She found herself thrown in here, there, and everywhere— she even did a week back with the hated chickens, and somehow she was too wound up to worry whether she got scratched or flown at by the roosters. When one attacked her, she kicked him with her rubber boot. He flew away squawking and left her to carry on with her work.

At night they listened to the radio and read the papers. Things were getting really scary. The papers showed photographs of rows and rows of Egyptian tanks, and Syrian planes, and Jordanian big guns, mustering on the borders all around them.

And still it wasn't war. Still there was hope that somehow it could be averted.

One day, as the crisis mounted to its climax, Lesley found a moment to climb the steps to the culture-house balcony.

She stood there with her hands on the rail, looking at the view. How had she ever been able to think of the river below her as just another river? Now it might as well have been a wall ten feet thick. She wished it were. There seemed to be nothing to protect them if the Jordanians decided to fight. But they might not. King Hussein wasn't at all friendly with President Nasser of Egypt. He probably wouldn't endanger his already poor country by starting trouble with the Israelis.

There were no more signs of farming on the far side. The farmers seemed to be holed up in their villages. Mustapha's father's orange grove was abandoned. But at least, thought Lesley, they, like the kibbutz, had got the citrus harvest in. It secretly pleased her to know that.

"Well, Mustapha," she said to him in Arabic, in her head, "are we going to be enemies now? What do you think?"

On the Israeli side, all was bustle and activity. Army trucks and jeeps were everywhere, together with excavators digging trenches and dugouts and gun emplacements. Khaki figures hurried purposefully about. The kibbutz fence was being strengthened. There was no way you could slip under it now.

Even as Lesley watched, a government excavator rumbled in through the main gates to begin digging a series of zigzag trenches on Moshe's lovingly tended lawns. How hard he had worked to reclaim this land from dust and sand and stones and thistles! The relentless teeth of the great machine bit into the green carpet—a work of destruction that might save their lives, when the bombs and shells started falling.

Lesley had stopped writing in her diary. There was no time. Any time she had for writing went on letters to Noah.

It was frustrating in one way. He never answered, and now more than ever she longed to hear from him. It was like stretching your hand across time and space, waiting in vain for a warm answering hand to take hold of it and grip it tightly. He was often in her thoughts these days as she watched the other kids' brothers. She wished he were here and in the army. How would he look in that rather casual uniform with a gun under his arm? How must he be feeling, safe in Saskatoon, watching all this on television?

Her letters to him were not always very tactful, but she wrote as she felt.

Darling Noah,

I suppose you're worried. Please don't be. I bet the media are playing it up like mad, but here it doesn't feel so bad, and we're not at all scared. Anyway, even though we're on the border, we're not in a dangerous locality. Everyone agrees about that. And we've got lovely safe air-raid shelters, and we've done drills to get down into them quickly. Guess who cleaned all the rubbish and dead leaves out of them, and even helped the carpenter make little bunks for the younger kids? I did.

I guess we're all doing stuff we never dreamed we could do. You should see Daddy! Lugging the newborn calves around in his arms and milking the whole herd by himself. He talks to them in English and Yiddish, and the local joke is they've started to moo with a Canadian accent!

As for Mom, she bumps out to the fields in a dirty old cattle truck and hacks down the bananas as if she were twenty years old. You remember how she'd never wear trousers cos she said they were unfeminine? Now she wears a pair of Dad's oldest "worker-blue" pants pulled in at the waist with an old belt, with one of my T-shirts and a kova tembel—like a dunce's cap—stuck on her hair, and I'm here to tell you she looks great.

I'm what's called a cork, I get stuck in wherever I'm needed. So far I've mucked out chickens, lugged bananas, cleaned out the shelters, washed ten million dishes in the kitchen, and been left to the mercies of eighteen six-year-olds for a whole afternoon. Give me the roosters every time—the little kids ate me for tea!

I hate to admit it, but I'm sort of enjoying the crisis, in a way. Funny how it brings out the best in people, everyone helping and joking and nobody grousing. Of course, if I were married or had someone close to me in the army, I guess I'd feel different.

You know I've been helping the kids a bit with English. Well, Shula, she's my best friend, has written a poem called "War" which I think is terrific. I'm copying it for you cos it gives a real feeling of what it's like, being here:

158

War!
What does that word mean?
I don't understand people.
Why must they fight?
Must we look now into Death's face?
My father, my brother,
And yours, and yours,
We say good-bye to them and wish them luck
As if they were going to an exam.
We smile at them and try to make jokes
And they go away in their new-old clothes.
But we are sending them into the mouth of Death.
We are sending them to be changed
Into killers.
My brother Rami is not a killer.
My father has never hurt anyone.
What will happen?
I'm frightened for my father and my brother!
Aren't you frightened, too?
Will we see them again?
Will we know them if we see them?
What is this thing called war?
What will it do to us all?

When Lesley had sent this off, on the twenty-third of May, she had a feeling she'd done wrong to send it. Maybe it would make Noah feel bad. But it was too late, and anyway she had too many things to think about to worry about it for long.

S I X T E E N

The Unexpected Happens

Baruch came dashing into the *kitta* one evening at the end of May.

"Nasser's closed the Strait of Tiran!" he shouted.

They rushed to the big map of the Middle East that Meir had hung on the back wall of their classroom. It was grubby from their fingermarks, and now eighteen forefingers prodded at it again.

"Look, there! See? It means our ships can't get into the Red Sea or use our port at Eilat! And it's meant to be an international waterway."

"*Casus belli!*" said Danny.

"What?"

"A cause for war."

"Rami says it's got to come," said Shula. Rami was home on leave for a few hours. He'd been down in the Negev Desert and was burned brown. "The soldiers always know. Rami says there can't *not* be a war, and that was before this about the Strait of Thing."

"It's nearly time—let's go and watch the news on television!"

The kibbutz had bought a communal set only two weeks before, the better to keep up with events. It was located in the culture house. They all rushed up there through the darkness. There were quite a number of kibbutz members, mainly older people, sitting on hard chairs in front of the set. They turned and shushed the group as it burst in. Subdued, they found chairs and settled down.

Lesley's Hebrew, though much improved, was not yet good enough to follow the news. But there was no misinterpreting the extraordinary image that appeared on the screen, which made everyone in the big room gasp.

It was nothing less than King Hussein of Jordan, and President Nasser of Egypt, embracing and kissing one another on both cheeks like a pair of Arab brothers.

She didn't have to ask Danny or Baruch for an explanation. These two old Arab enemies, who had been abusing each other for years, whose mutual hatred gave Israel one of its own safeguards, had buried the hatchet. The commentary was talking in doom-laden tones about a pact. An anti-Israel pact. The two countries were clearly going to work in unison to defeat Israel.

After the news finished, the kibbutzniks walked out into

the darkness in dazed silence. Only Baruch rattled on, almost in triumph, it seemed, at having prophesied aright. The Jordanian Arab Legion was the best army the Arabs had—British-trained, British-officered. And the Egyptians, armed by the Russians, were very powerful. Syria, Lebanon, possibly Iraq—they would all be happy to join in, if there seemed a good chance of an Arab victory and a division of the spoils. Once again, as in 1948, Israel faced a combined assault, and possible disaster.

Lesley didn't go back with the others. As often in times of stress, she headed for her parents' flat.

They were in their dressing gowns, ready for bed, and Lesley's mother was just making a cup of cocoa. Her father was struggling with a Hebrew newspaper.

"Did you see the news on TV, Les?" he asked.

"Yup," she said grimly. Her parents looked at her expectantly. "Dear Gamel Abdul and dear Hussie snogging away on the tarmac at Cairo like a pair of lovebirds. As they hugged each other, you could almost see the daggers they wished they were sticking in each other's backs." This was Baruch's remark, not hers, but it was too good not to use.

Her parents exchanged alarmed glances. Lesley felt proud, in an awful sort of way, to be bringing them the news. She told them about the pact.

"It sounds bad," said her father. "Les, what are you doing there?"

"Opening the shutters. It's so darned hot in here."

"I wouldn't, kiddo. We shouldn't show too much light."

"There's no blackout yet."

"But there's going to be," said her mother. "We got our

162

order of blackout material today—mountains of it—and tomorrow we're cutting out lengths. Every household will get enough to black out their windows."

There was a light knock on the outer door, leading to the porch. Lesley went to see who was there. It was Ayala. She took Lesley mysteriously by the wrist and drew her outside.

"Lesley," she said in a low voice, "there is someone in the office who wants to see you."

The soldier! The one who had seen them—that time! Otherwise why did Ayala sound so serious? "Who—who is it?"

"I'll tell you as we go. Just tell your parents something so they don't worry."

"You mean a lie?"

"You can decide later what to tell them. Just fob them off for the moment."

Lesley felt very alarmed. What could this be? Ayala was kindly in her gruff way, but she wouldn't cover up for Lesley if she was in trouble.

"Go on, hurry up."

Lesley turned back into the flat. "I have to go somewhere," she awkwardly. "I'll be right back."

"Is anything wrong?"

"No—I don't think so. See you."

She ducked out hastily before they could ask more. Ayala led her quickly along the paths to the main office block. Lesley noticed that the lamps beside the paths had been dimmed to a glow. Ayala carried a flashlight that she didn't use.

"Is it bad news?" Lesley asked.

"You might think it's just the opposite."

"Why? What is it? Oh, do tell me!"

"Perhaps I'll let you see for yourself."

They arrived. There were already blackout curtains on the office windows, and every pane of glass had a thick Union Jack pattern of brown sticky paper pasted to it.

"What's that for?"

"So the glass won't shatter in a blast," said Ayala shortly. "Come on."

There was a lot of unusual noise going on inside the office. As they entered, Lesley was surprised to see a crowd of strangers—all young men—in the outer office. They all seemed just to have arrived, and carried rucksacks, suitcases, and cameras. They were an odd mixture of types. Some were obviously Jewish, but there were a couple who looked quite Scandinavian, and there was one black man. They wore an assortment of jeans, jackets or sweatshirts with university insignia on them, open-necked shirts, and all sorts of headgear. There were one or two in suits. The general effect was of a group of tourists from all over the world. Several of them talked with American accents. And there was an atmosphere of keyed-up excitement.

"What's all this?" Lesley asked Ayala as they pushed their way through to the door of the inner office.

"Volunteers," said Ayala. "Haven't you heard? They're flooding in from all over the world. Mostly Jewish, of course, but others, too, surprisingly enough."

"But what for? What do they want?"

"To help us. To fight for us." Ayala gave her a quick look over her shoulder and added in Hebrew, "To die for

164

us if necessary." She said, "Excuse me," to a tall blond boy leaning against the door. He jumped aside and pulled it open for her. Again Ayala took Lesley's hand and pulled her through the crush into the relative emptiness of the secretary's office.

"Phew!" said Lesley. "What a scrum—"

And then she saw Noah.

He was sitting quietly on a bench under the window. He stood up as he saw her and stood looking at her.

"Noah . . . ?" she asked in a soft, incredulous voice.

"Yep, it's me."

He looked very pale compared with the Bet She'an Valley tan everyone else had, but his face was more than just untanned. It was white. He wore casual clothes and carried luggage like the others outside. Like the volunteers . . .

She started to tremble, and right there in front of the secretary of the kibbutz and Ayala she burst into tears. Noah hugged her tightly.

"Sh, sis, it's okay."

"Oh, Noah—you came—"

"I couldn't not, I guess."

A pang of glad guilt struck her. "Was it my letter that—"

"Not really. Just sort of put the final kibosh on everything that had been pushing me anyhow."

"You're with them? A—a volunteer?"

"If you'll have me."

Lesley looked through her tears at the kibbutz secretary. He was a tall, white-haired man with stooped shoulders and a worried look that never seemed to leave his leathery face.

165

"Your brother's told us the situation," he said. "It's not our business really. We're accepting twenty volunteers. If you think your parents wouldn't object, we'll accept him with the others. To us he's another welcome pair of hands."

Lesley turned wide eyes back to Noah's anxious, waiting face.

"But what if—what if they do object?"

"That's for them to decide, don't you think?" said Ayala quietly.

"But it'll be such a shock! You don't know! It'll be as if he was coming back from the dead!"

Noah pushed his hand through his tousled hair in a gesture she remembered from years ago. "I couldn't not come," he repeated. "Won't they understand? You weren't kidding when you said about the media playing it up. From where I sat, it looked as if—as if you didn't stand a chance over here, as if you were all going to be massacred—"

Ayala laid her hand on his arm.

"Don't say things like that here," she said, gently but somehow sternly.

"I'm sorry," said Noah humbly. "But you don't know what I've been through. I haven't slept properly for weeks. I couldn't work—"

"What about your job?"

"I quit."

"Quit your *job*?"

"I couldn't concentrate. I was no use to them."

"But they'll take you back afterward?"

166

Noah gazed at her with bewildered eyes. "Is there going to be an afterward?"

"Enough already!" snapped the secretary suddenly. "Of course there'll be an afterward! You think there's going to be *no more Israel*? We'll win because of our secret weapon."

Lesley and Noah looked at him with wild, unreasoning hope.

"A secret weapon? Are you sure?"

"Sure I am sure."

"What is it?"

"We have no alternative."

Noah went limp and gave a choked laugh. "That's a catch phrase from the forty-eight war, for God's sake—I thought you meant a real weapon."

"It was a real weapon then, and so it is now. You'll see. Now go on, out of here and make some decision. I've got work to do."

Lesley and Noah pushed their way out through the crowd of strangers. Outside the building they stood in the pine-scented darkness, their faces lit by a lone lamp. Noah looked even more strained and somehow unearthly, like a phantom. "The spirit of Christmas Past," Lesley spluttered suddenly. "That's what you look like!"

"Passover Past, maybe," said Noah thinly. "What's that noise?"

"Frogs. What are we going to *do*, Noah? What *are* we going to do?"

"I don't know. I could never plan beyond just—getting here."

"What about Donna?" she remembered suddenly.

167

Noah turned his face away. "I left her at home."

"Not without telling her?"

"Of *course* not! What do you take me for? We talked for hours—days."

"And she agreed? She let you come?"

"I guess—like Israel—she had no alternative."

"But didn't she try to stop you?"

Noah said nothing for a moment. He stood with his profile turned to her.

"Les," he said, "I've spent a lot of years trying to push the Jew in me down deep enough so I could live like anybody. It was like trying to change shape. You can't. And when this crisis started, my buried Jew just jumped up and took me over, and not being blind or stupid, Donna saw it. She loves me, I guess. She saw I was—what I was going through. All we talked about was the danger, me going into danger."

"She wanted to keep you there to be safe."

"No. She wanted to come with me."

"Wow," said Lesley, her notion of Donna changing in an instant. "And she's not even a Jew."

They stood silently, holding hands. The door of the office burst open and the volunteers came out, talking earnestly to each other. Lesley said, "Go with them."

"What about the folks? Will you tell them?"

Lesley shivered.

"I'll try. I don't promise. Go with the others for now. I'll find you tomorrow morning and let you know what's happening."

He kissed her. "Aren't you scared?" he said. "You don't look scared."

168

"I'm scared rigid of Dad right now. I'm not scared about the war."

"How come?"

"I don't know, Noah. You feel safe here, as if nothing could happen as long as you're all together."

"Maybe you don't know how bad things are."

"Enough already. Don't be defeatist. Look, your buddies are halfway down the hill. Go." She hit him on the back.

He went. She watched him run after the others with his rucksack bumping. He thought he'd come here to die. . . . Lesley shrugged a little. She wanted to stop him being afraid, but there was no way she could do it. She guessed it would stop by itself. It was wonderful to see him, but somehow she felt a tiny bit disappointed. She had imagined having a brother like the others, confident, strong, unselfconsciously brave, standing like a rock in their defense.

Now she saw that she would have to be his rock for a little while, till he got used to being an Israeli.

SEVENTEEN

Meeting

Lesley reached her parents' door, and stopped cold.

All the way down from the office, she'd tried to rehearse the scene. She'd walk boldly in and announce Noah's arrival directly, she'd drop hints, try making them guess. . . . Stupid. Hopeless. The thing he'd given her to do was a simple impossibility.

Standing outside the screen door, she remembered Mustapha, how he had stopped on his side of the river, unable to force his body to obey him. Was her father, then, still the "enemy"? No. She loved him now more than ever before, and she wasn't afraid of him or angry with him for bringing her here. But he was weird about Noah; it went so deep it reached and awakened a different Nat Shelby, someone she didn't understand or recognize. How would he react if he ever found out she had contacted Noah in Saskatoon?

She uttered an Arabic curse learned from Gadi (who didn't know what it meant any more than she did) and crept away, ashamed of her cowardice.

It was getting late, but the kids were mostly still up, listening to the latest news on the class radio. It was all about Hussein's visit to Cairo, world reactions to the crisis, the Israeli government's troubles.

"Talk about lack of unity," grumbled Baruch. "Put two Jewish politicians together, and who needs any Arabs?"

"Why don't they let Moshe Dayan take over as Minister for Defense?" fretted Naomi. "Then we'd get some action."

"Then it'd be 'good-bye to peace,' " said Shula. *"Shalom"* meant "peace" as well as "hello" and "good-bye," so it came out as *"shalom to shalom."*

Esther and Aviva came in. Everyone turned to look at them—they were actually *giggling.*

"What's so funny?" asked Ofer sourly.

"Chevrai, have you *seen* the volunteers?" Esther said, grinning.

"What volunteers? What are you talking?"

"Hundreds of lovely heroes from abroad," said Aviva. "You've never seen such 'pieces,' just not normal!" (This was the sabras' way of saying something or somebody was special.)

"Especially that red-haired one from Canada," said Esther. "Thanks, Leslee, for teaching me English! Now I can talk to him. His name's Garry. *Ya-va-yay!*" She went into a little dance.

"Don't make fools out of yourselves," said Amnon. "They won't bother with a pair of babies like you two. You'd better stick to us little boys for a bit longer." He wrapped a plump arm around each of their necks and tried to kiss both their cheeks at once, which made them scream and cuff him, and effectively broke up the somber group around the radio.

When they were all in bed, Lesley, who could contain herself no longer, leaned over toward Shula and whispered, "Shula, guess what."

"What."

"My brother's here."

Shula rolled over so sharply she nearly fell out of bed. "What do you say! I never knew you had a brother!"

"Oh, *sheket,*" mumbled Ofer, who was nearly asleep.

"He married a Catholic girl and my father threw him out of the family," whispered Lesley.

"What for?" whispered Shula in amazement.

"He—converted. Became a Catholic." Shula just stared at her through the half-darkness. "He stopped being a Jew."

"How? If he is one?"

"He changed his religion."

"Oh—*religion,*" said Shula in a bored voice. "That's all *shtut.* All it ever does is cause trouble. But what's the fuss? I suppose he only did it to marry his girl. I heard about a girl in another kibbutz who wanted to marry an Arab, and

172

she became a Muslim. But of course she was still Jewish really."

"In Canada, being Jewish *means* religion."

"*Shtuyot!* If being Jewish means being religious-Jewish, then none of us are Jewish, I suppose. Has your father stopped being a Jew because he doesn't keep the *mitzvot* and all that *shtut* anymore?"

Lesley lay back and thought. *What,* she asked herself, *is a Jew? If you're a Jew because your parents are Jewish, then Noah was still a Jew. But Daddy says he's not, and he can't bear having a son who isn't a Jew. But all Noah did was to change his religion—which wasn't much of a change because he was never very religious anyway. And he never really believed in all the Catholic things.*

"I expect Daddy still believes in God," she said slowly, trying to work it all out.

"Does he *really*?" said Shula incredulously.

"Why not?" said Lesley. "I bet some of the other parents do, too, in their hearts."

"Well, not mine!"

"Anyhow, Daddy doesn't practice his religion anymore, or he couldn't live here. He's left all that behind. He seems to think living in Israel is—is religion enough."

"Quite right!" said Shula forcefully.

"So if he thinks it's religion that makes you a Jew or not a Jew," Lesley went on, "then he's no more Jewish now than Noah."

She sat up in bed sharply.

"Shula! That's it! That must be right. How can he argue with that?"

173

"Oh, parents can always argue!"

"But it's not fair!"

"If your father was fair, he'd never have thrown your brother out in the first place." She rolled over again. "Can't wait to see him. Is he a *gever*? Will Esther and Aviva think he's a 'piece,' like this Garry?"

"Well—he wears glasses."

"My father wears glasses. You can wear glasses and still be a *gever.*"

Next morning, Lesley awoke very early and crept out before the others were stirring. It was summer in the valley, and the sun was up. There was no dew these mornings because even the nights were warm.

The kibbutz was wide awake. The tractors, bulldozers, and excavators were busy on the earthworks. The beauty of the morning was entirely spoiled by the awful roaring and grinding of the machines, and the sights of ruined lawns and jagged scars in the ground reminded her far more of the coming war than the uniforms and small arms she was used to seeing.

Lesley paused briefly beside a huge pit that was being dug for a new shelter which, Baruch had assured them, couldn't possibly be ready in time. He said it would make a good mass grave. Lesley shivered and hurried on.

She'd decided in the night what had to be done. She would go to the *refet* where her father worked from 4 A.M., and there among the cows and other workers, where he couldn't throw himself into a real fit, she would just come out with it. *"Noah's come, he's one of the volunteers."* After that, whatever would happen would happen.

174

On the way to the farm she passed a path that led to the rather tumble-down wooden huts where the first settlers had lived before permanent housing was built. These were now used to house work parties of youngsters from the towns. Probably that was where the volunteers would have been sent to sleep.

Perhaps she would just nip along there and see where Noah was, have a word with him before the dreaded encounter with her father.

Suddenly she heard the sound of the little garden tractor and saw her father driving it from the cowsheds. The trailer at the back was loaded with milk churns. He was bringing the morning milk to the kitchen.

Before she could duck out of sight, he'd seen her and veered the tractor in her direction. She felt her stomach begin to turn over. She would have to tell him now, out here, *now.* . . . Oh, why hadn't she done it last night! Then he could have slept on it, and in any case it would be over.

With the tractor a few yards from her, she suddenly heard footsteps coming along the path from the huts. With an awful feeling of inevitability, she turned her head.

Yes, it was Noah! Her father couldn't see him because the path ran off at right angles between high hedges. Father and son were approaching each other along a collision course with her at its meeting point.

She stepped back.

Nat Shelby stopped the tractor and said cheerily, "Hi, kiddo, what are you doing up so—"

And then Noah walked around the corner.

The two men did not actually collide. But their looks

did. At the moment and the place where they met, something happened like a silent, invisible explosion. The bitter words, the years, the passions, the regrets—all struck, burst, and scattered like hard, clear, broken bubbles when Noah and Nat saw each other.

Something happened to Nat's face when he saw his son again that was quite new in Lesley's experience of him. It sagged and grew suddenly old and gray as if the life had been knocked right out of his body. It seemed unnatural that he could still keep sitting there upright on the tractor, his hands resting on the wheel and the engine running like the only live thing on the scene.

Noah, too, was rigid and white in the face.

Her eyes flashing from one to the other of them, Lesley's guilt at the secret meetings, her burden of responsibility, melted away. She saw suddenly this was not her business at all. This was something stronger and deeper than she was yet old enough to grasp. She felt she should just disappear and leave them together, and she did edge backward into the shadow of the hedge so as to be out of their picture of each other.

Noah recovered first, because he had been prepared.

"Hello, Dad," he said very quietly.

"Hello, son," answered their father with some uncertainty like a question mark in his voice. And then he seemed to shrink into himself, and dropped his head between his shoulders, and his hands gripped the wheel so hard that not only the knuckles, but all the fingers went livid with the effort to control his trembling.

After a moment he threw up his head and said in a voice

176

too loud to be as normal as he wanted, "What are you doing in this—neck of the woods?"

"Can we talk, Dad?"

"Not now," said this old man whom Lesley couldn't quite recognize. "I'm working."

"I've been assigned to work in the *refet* with you."

Nat looked bewildered. He couldn't grasp what was happening. "How—how did that happen?" he asked.

"I asked to be," said Noah.

"Did you say—*refet*?"

"Yes."

"So soon you know some Hebrew?"

"I've been learning it a long time."

"Have you," said Nat dazedly. "Have you."

His eyes were on the ground. Lesley, still watching from her shadow, thought: *He looks ashamed. He can't remember what it was all about. He can't feel his anger anymore.* She knew about wanting to go on being angry and not being able to. She felt her heart go out to him, but she didn't move. She couldn't break in and spoil it.

"Those shoes are no good to you," Nat said unsteadily. "You'll be in muck to the knees. I'll fix you up with some proper boots."

Noah was moving. He was walking forward until he stood beside his father, who, with a great effort it seemed, got off the tractor. Lesley saw his eyes come up slowly from the ground, and meet Noah's, and then their hands came up toward each other.

And then she couldn't watch for another second. She couldn't bear it. She turned away in a flash and ran, and ran, blinded by tumultuous feelings. So blinded that she didn't look where she was going, only seeing at the last moment that she was on the brink of one of the new trenches. She just managed to jump down into it instead of falling.

There, on the hard, sandy bottom marked with the teeth of the excavator, she sat down, hidden from everyone, and let out her feelings in great gasping outbursts of laughter and tears.

EIGHTEEN

Cull Before the Storm

Lesley wasn't there when her father took Noah home for the first time. When she got back at lunchtime, she found the three of them: Noah and Nat in their work clothes and boots, dirt all over the floor—unheard of, her father always changed in the *refet*—sitting on the sofa looking worn out with something more than just work, while her mother sat opposite them, staring at Noah in exhausted silence.

One look at her mother's face told Lesley she had cried till she had no tears left, and now she looked just empty. But on her smooth, drained face was a look of calm, and the shadow of a great happiness that was

179

going to burst upon her as soon as she had strength to feel it.

They all looked around as Lesley came in. Her mother lifted her hand as if it were very heavy and held it out to her. Lesley took it, and they all just looked at each other, except that Miriam looked only at Lesley. She held her hand very tightly and said in a choked voice, "Thank you, darling. Thank you."

"What for, Mom?"

"Noah's told us. He—this wouldn't have happened except for you."

Lesley looked quickly, scaredly, at her father.

"You're not mad at me?"

Her father shook his head and smiled a little, a smile with a lot of pain left in it. Her mother held her around the waist and pressed her face against her.

"How could we be mad at you—now?"

A week can pass like a flash, or it can go on forever. But this particular week seemed to do both.

It hurtled past as far as preparations for war were concerned. These went on day and night, and the work of the kibbutz had to go on, too, no matter what might be going on in people's private lives. Every person of any age capable of work—including Ofer's sister Yocheved, who was expecting a baby at any moment—worked almost every hour they were awake, and some when, it seemed to Lesley, they were more than half-asleep. There was no time to feel afraid, or even to think much.

But at home on the rare occasions when the family

180

managed to be together, time slowed to a crawl. Five minutes standing in the porch exchanging a few words or drinking a cup of coffee was like time out of time, endless moments of stillness snatched from the rush and tumble of life outside.

It was a long time before things began to be natural between them. Too much misunderstanding, too much anger and pain had to be talked through and overcome. And it was hard to talk. Polite chat was impossible, and words were hard to find for the deep-rooted things that had to be discussed. So there were silences, and it was these that made the time pass so slowly. It was hard to be together, and hard to be apart, and the crisis made a fierce, jagged background for their private struggle to relearn each other and heal old wounds.

Noah was soon taken out of the *refet* and put to other work—work that maddened him because it seemed to have nothing to do with the war. For two days he actually had to act as lifeguard at the swimming pool. He could hardly believe that people were still going to swim, but the kibbutzniks were trying to keep as much normality in daily life as possible, and besides, swimming was a blessing in that fiery weather. But Noah had come to fight for his family, and it was intolerable to spend hours lounging by the pool with a whistle around his neck, getting a beautiful tropical tan.

"Couldn't they use me, Dad?" he kept asking. "They're building air-raid shelters here! Drainage, ventilation—this is my *field*, for Pete's sake!" But the government was building the shelters; the designs were fixed. Engineers weren't needed, just the builders, and even they were from outside.

"Couldn't I join the army? I can shoot!" But at that the kibbutzniks only smiled tolerantly. Foreigners were not allowed to join up. Being "able to shoot" was scarcely enough to be eligible for one of the best fighting forces in the world. Noah's frustration added to the tensions at home.

But family tensions were overwhelmed by the wider ones. Beyond the borders, in Egypt, Syria, and Jordan, the Arabs were building up their forces. The television showed the tanks, the artillery, the marching men, the leaders embracing, all buddies now. Israel's friends in the West did what they claimed was their best. Diplomats rushed from capital to capital, promises were made and broken, initiatives put forward and abandoned. It was plain to everyone in Israel that when the fighting started, they would stand alone.

In the *kitta,* at night, the boys tuned in to the Arab radio stations. The voices raved and ranted. They sounded mad with rage, with bloodthirstiness. The odd few words the group could catch seemed to carry more menace than if they had understood it all.

Worn out with work and tension, they would crawl to bed, but not always to sleep. They were thinking of their loved ones. Rami had gone again; so had Ofer's brother-in-law Brosh, and Aviva's father. . . . Once or twice Shula reached out her hand across the space between her bed and Lesley's and Lesley clutched it. It was so good to have other people in the room, to have Ofer to say bluffly, in his newly growly voice, "Listen, they don't know us! We'll show them, you wait! Brosh says we can do it." He was a good antidote to Baruch's relentless pessimism.

Sometimes lying there in the semi-dark, hot under a single sheet, Lesley let herself dream of Rami, handsome grown-up Rami, shielding her from harm. But as she dropped to sleep at last, it was Ofer's hand she wanted to hold.

Early on the fifth of June, Lesley was sweeping out the bedroom. She could hear a radio droning faintly from the classroom. English first lesson again—since Meir left, they'd had English half the time, which meant Lesley didn't have to go to lessons and had to help Adda with the housework. She was sweeping sand and bits of junk out from under Ofer's bed, when she felt something—like a shock wave from an explosion before you hear it. It sent a shiver down her back. She straightened up, and a second later she heard a shout from the classroom.

She rushed into the corridor. No shouting now, but an acute, listening silence pierced by the voice on the radio, now turned up loud. She ran to the classroom. The group around the radio, which was on the teacher's desk, was like a football scrum, all backs, no heads.

"What is it, has it started?" she cried.

Everyone said, "Sh!" But Shula's head came out of the scrum, all red, her red hair in a bush.

"The lousy damn war has begin!" she said. "Do you wish you was in Skaskapoon?"

"No!" Lesley almost shouted.

"Nut case," said Shula. "Come and listen. I translate."

Lesley listened. The Egyptians had moved their troops forward, and the Israelis had met them in a head-on battle, which was raging hundreds of miles to the south. Shula's red face turned pale and she bit her nails. Lesley automatically reached to pull her hand down, but stopped. Rami was in the south.

Many of the others lost the first feeling of excitement—relief, almost, that it had started, that the waiting was over—and began to realize what it meant for their fathers and brothers. Ofer hurried away. Lesley guessed where to. Yocheved, with Brosh far away and her baby due, must be terribly upset. He wanted to be with her.

One by one the kids started to move off, to be with family or find some work to do. But suddenly there was a bang as the outside door closed sharply, and the voice of their English teacher rang through the building.

"Where do you all think you're off to? Don't you know you've got an English lesson?"

A babble of voices brought her up to date on the situation, but she interrupted on a note of authority.

"But children! *Children!* I know all that. It makes no difference to our schedule. Now, come along—into class at once. Get out your *New Horizons* and open to page eighty-three!"

A groan went up from a dozen throats, but she was not to be swayed. Grumbling loudly, most of the class settled into their seats.

"What a stupid idea!"

"Who could learn today?"

"To all the winds with English at a time like this!"

184

But after a few minutes they were all bent over their books, and the war and its terrors took a back seat in their minds for the length of the lesson. For the first time, Lesley was asked to join in.

"I need a little help today" was how the teacher put it.

Lesley sat at the front and gave definitions of new words and answered questions on grammar. She thought at the time the teacher was being unreasonable, that the lesson was irrelevant and infuriating. Later she wasn't so sure.

Even the English teacher, though, couldn't contain the class for more than two periods. They grew restless, wanting to turn on the radio, go outside, see what was going on. At last she said, "All right, then. Be off with you." And they rose like a flock of birds and scattered.

Lesley went to the bedroom and fumbled for her key. All during the lesson she'd been thinking of her diary. She would write about the war. This was the first bit of real history she'd ever lived through, and she was going to record it, and her feelings about it, vivid and firsthand, as events unfolded.

NINETEEN

War Diary

June 5: War's begun! Heavy fighting in the desert. Shula's simply sick with worry about Rami. Is he there? David's father is—he's an officer in tanks. So's Brosh, Yocheved's husband. She went into hospital in Afula this afternoon to have her baby (no news yet). Baruch, of *course,* said it's good she's having it now, all the hospitals will be full of wounded in a few days. He *would.*

Listened to Cairo Radio this morning, broadcasting in Hebrew, trying to depress our morale. Their *Ivrit* was full of funny mistakes, like saying, "Our soldiers are advancing on all bras" (*khasiot*) instead of "on all fronts" (*khasitot*). The boys roared. Cairo Radio also said

Haifa and Tel Aviv had been completely wiped out. What's the point of telling such lies? But our radio must be lying, too, because *it* said our air force has destroyed the whole Egyptian air force on the ground. Just too good to be true! It would mean we hadn't even had to kill their pilots. But if it isn't true, why haven't they bombed anywhere?

Maybe they have, and we haven't been told. I do want to think our side's telling us the truth.

Worked all afternoon in *gan yud* with Shula. The little kids in the *gan* are all terribly keyed up. They can't grasp what's happening, but of course they know something is. Practiced taking them down the shelter, "putting them to bed" in the little built-in bunks. They loved it!

I hope the Jordanians don't join in the fighting. Baruch says King Hussein won't be able to keep out of it because of the stupid pact.

June 6: Still absolutely quiet here. It's weird. But there's fighting going on on practically every other border. The Jordanians *have* joined in. Really sad. Also dangerous. Danny says they're the best fighters of any of the Arabs. There's something pretty fierce going on around Jerusalem. Daddy said, with a kind of wild look in his eyes, "If only we could get the Old City back!" What's so important is the Western Wall of the old Temple. It's our holiest place. The only Jews who've been able to visit it since 1948 (when the Jordanian Arab Legion captured it) have been Western tourists. Baruch says we'll have to pull the City down stone by stone to take it away from the Legion.

It's terrible to think of the fighting that's going on so close to us while we sit here so quietly with everything almost normal. Well—except for the blackout, and everybody worried sick about somebody. Farther north the Syrians are shelling the valley settlements. They always have, the odd shell, but now it's a real barrage. Sometimes I think I can hear rumbling on gusts of wind. They're attacking on the ground, too—trying to reach Kibbutz Dan. All the boys are fretting because nothing "exciting" is happening here, and all the girls (except Naomi!) think they're crazy not to be grateful.

Yocheved's had a boy. Ofer's quite excited. She's going to call him Shalom. How awful having a baby when your husband's in a battle.

No news of any of *our* soldiers yet, but they must be fighting wonderfully. The Egyptians are being pushed back on all "bras"! Oh—how could I forget to mention it first? It was *true* about our bombing all their planes! Esther's cousin's a pilot—he must have taken part in that operation. We're all terribly excited absolutely every minute. We can't believe it's all real.

But of course, as Baruch keeps reminding us, things can easily turn against us.

June 7: Terrible news. Baruch's brother Avri has been wounded. We don't know how badly. His parents live next door to Mom and Dad. His poor mother's nearly crazy. He's in hospital in Beersheba. It's far to the south, but they've both gone straight off there. We won't know more till they come back.

Yocheved and her baby were sent home from the hospital. They're clearing all the nonserious cases out to make room for wounded from the Jordanian front, which is very, very hot. We've taken a lot of the big bulge of land on the West Bank of the Jordan, just south of us. I'm quite sure I can hear noises now when the wind blows from the south. There's a rumor that we've captured Ramallah and Jenin, two big towns there. But most of the attention is on the battle for Jerusalem. By tonight it may have fallen to us!

(Later) Danny's father came along to the *kitta* and gave us a talk about the situation. He's in the reserve, but they haven't called him up yet because he's got a bad back.

He says, whatever else we do, we've got to take the Golan Heights. That's the high bit just over the Syrian border where their army is dug in all along the ridge and has been shelling the kibbutzim underneath them for years. Our planes are bombing them now, and Danny's father says that now we've taken Sharm al-Sheikh (that's where the Egyptians stopped our ships getting into the Gulf of Aqaba, which is what the war really started about), a lot of our men will come up from the desert and attack the Heights. It will be terribly hard. It means the infantry climbing right up a practically sheer cliff under the Syrian bunkers, right into their guns.

The Syrians have been the worst about saying what they were going to do to us. One of their broadcasts said (I can hardly write this, it's so horrible) they were going to pave the road from Damascus to Tel Aviv with the skulls of Jewish children. I sort of hate them when I think about that, and how they've never left our settlements in peace,

189

all these years. I don't hate the Egyptians. I feel sorry for them in a way—them screaming lies at us over the radio is kind of pathetic. As for the Jordanians, of course I don't hate them. I even like their little King, and as for the people—well, when I think of them, I just see Mustapha riding away on Eeyore. Of course, I know they're not all like him, but most of them are so poor! I bet Eeyore never tasted chocolate again, or Mustapha either. . . . I wonder where he is? I wonder if he hates me. Baruch says Arab kids are taught to hate us in school. The way they learn math for instance is "If there are ten Jews and you kill three, how many are left?" I think that's fairly disgusting.

We've heard from a lot of our men. Something great happens here. When the soldiers pass through a town, lots of people come out to cheer them and give them soft drinks and candy. Then the soldiers give them bits of paper with their names and home phone numbers scribbled on them. Then the person goes off and phones the soldier's home and says, "I've seen him, he's okay and sends his love." I've seen a few mothers getting these messages in the middle of work. Rina, who's Aviva's aunt, quite old now, has gone back to the sheep where she worked when she was younger. When her message came, she just picked up a half-grown lamb and did a funny clumsy dance. Others burst into tears of relief.

June 8: We went to bed early last night because the excitement makes us all tired, and woke up this morning to wonderful news. We've taken the Old City. The whole country's going mad with joy! They say we've reached the

Suez Canal as well, which means we've taken the whole of the Sinai Desert and don't have to be afraid anymore of all those awful rockets the Egyptians had there, aimed at our cities.

The way it's all going so well, and so *quickly,* is making the Egyptians say the Americans and British are helping us. Ha, ha, fat chance. Anyway, as Moshe Dayan said, we don't want any other country's soldiers to die for us.

Shula told me a secret. She prayed last night, "Please, God, take care of Rami." She says she knows there's no one to hear, but she had to do something.

Aviva's father's home. He was wounded when his tank ran over a mine, but it's not serious, so that's one less to worry about. But it's awful about Avri. He's lost his foot. . . . Can't write about it, can't think about it. All Baruch can say is "If only that's the worst."

June 9: The worst day so far, though the war is going so well nobody can quite believe it. We *have* reached the Canal—our soldiers actually went swimming in it. We've taken the whole of the West Bank, and Jerusalem, and now only the Syrians have to be finished with.

But something dreadful has happened. We heard about it this morning. Even now I can't get my mind around it. Danny's father came and called Ofer out of the lesson. He didn't come back, but after a while somebody came and told the rest of us. Brosh has been killed.

We were just stunned. We all knew him really well. He was works manager, the one who decides where everyone should work, so there's no one in the kibbutz who didn't talk to him within the last ten days. Shula and Aviva and some of the others just couldn't stop crying, but I only cried when I saw Ofer. He came back into our room in the evening after being with Yocheved and her baby all day, trying to comfort her and Brosh's mother. He looked completely broken. He'd been crying, too. I couldn't help it, I just put my arms around him, and then Shula and Aviva did, too, and we all stood there together and cried. Ofer loved Brosh almost as much as his real brother, Adam.

To make everything worse, there's a rumor that Adam's at the Heights. If anything happened to him! No, I won't think about it.

A military escort brought Brosh's body back to the kibbutz in the afternoon. The whole kibbutz went to the funeral except a few people who had to look after the youngest children. It was so moving I could hardly stand it. All us kids walked together, wearing our Movement shirts and carrying the wreath we'd made, out to the cemetery, which is outside the fence in a little grove of trees.

Yocheved didn't come, of course, but Ofer's parents did, and Brosh's mother. She's a widow and Brosh was her only child. I couldn't keep from looking at her. You couldn't imagine how she must be feeling. You felt you shouldn't look, but you had to. She wore an ordinary Shabbat dress with no sleeves (it's unbearably hot) and her sunglasses, and Ofer's father stood close to her at the graveside and held her arm.

Ofer stood on the other side of her. He looked so tall and straight, my heart gave a sort of lurch when I looked at him. She looked as if she'd fall down if they let go of her.

A lot of people cried the whole time, but she didn't. She just kind of leaned forward as they took the coffin off the back of the open army truck and lowered it into the grave.

Then different people spoke about him and an army rabbi droned something (people in the kibbutz don't like the rabbis because they always try to force the country to be more religious, and you could feel nobody wanted to listen to him—he hadn't even known Brosh and the prayers meant nothing at all) and then came the most awful part. The escort fired a salute into the air and everybody jumped because it was like hearing the shots that killed him.

Then Ofer's father came forward as the oldest male relative and shoveled some earth into the grave, and Ofer had to hold Brosh's mother's arm by himself. When she heard the earth falling on the coffin, she seemed to shrink into herself. But she kept standing upright and she didn't make a sound, though there were a lot of other groans and Ofer's mother gave a sort of gasping cry, the saddest sound I've ever heard.

Ofer came to put in the next spadeful, standing there alone on the mound of earth. I can't describe how I felt when I saw him standing there. He gave a sob and I sobbed, too, at the same moment. Then our men, those that are still at home, came in turn and helped fill up the grave. The boys in our group did, too, because they're like Ofer's brothers. Gadi shoveled his in so fiercely. We could all see he was kind of raging.

Then three girls in uniform from Brosh's regiment came forward with a wreath, and afterward everyone who'd brought flowers laid them on the grave. We did, too. The earth looked so raw, somehow. Most of the earth here is light-colored and dry; the grave looked like a thick scar. I couldn't believe Brosh was lying dead underneath, that we'd never see him again.

I had to help Shula home. She just couldn't see for crying. She's lying with her back to me now, in bed, still crying. I know it's partly because she's more and more frightened about Rami, even though he's in Jerusalem and the fighting there is practically over.

How could I ever have been so stupid and unfeeling as to want Noah to fight? I'm so thankful every day that I can see him and touch him and know he's safe. Poor, poor Yocheved. Poor little Shalom. *God,* it's so horrible.

Amnon has just put his head in with the latest news. The Syrians are running. If only nobody else of ours is hurt or killed.

June 10: Midnight. The war is over! Just six days, and we've beaten them all. Every Arab country that was fighting us has agreed to a cease-fire, even Syria. It's like a dream, or a miracle.

How could we have won at all, let alone in six days? Despite Avri, and Brosh, and all the other horrors we've heard about, there's a feeling of triumph, almost of exultation. Aviva's grandfather, Abba Asher, keeps saying it's the hand of God. Lots of the old people—the parents' parents—are still religious. But the funny thing is, Shula's father, who's probably the most passionate atheist in the whole kibbutz, actually had tears in his eyes when news came that we'd taken the Old City, and over the radio we could hear the sound of the ram's horn being blown beside the Wall for the first time in twenty years. Shula told me she'd laughed and asked him what a wall of old stones mattered to him, but he'd turned on her quite angrily and told her not to dare laugh at what she didn't understand.

Daddy is ecstatic. He says it's the greatest thing for the Jewish people in a thousand years, apart from the founding of Israel, and that I'm lucky to be alive for this day. I thought he meant lucky not to have been killed, but he meant lucky to be living in this period of history.

Now I suppose everything will get back to normal and seem rather dull. I still can't believe I've been through a real war. In Saskatoon, it would have been just pictures on TV, with Dad and Mom wringing their hands helplessly and me getting irritated because I couldn't feel enough. . . . Soon the men will be back, and Meir, and Moshe, I'll be back working in the *noi,* and school will start again properly and . . . ho hum! But there are exciting things to look forward to.

We'll go on trips to see the Old City, and Golan, and Hebron, and all the other places our army captured. Maybe even the Suez Canal! We'll have to go quickly before the Arabs make peace and we give it all back. All except Jerusalem. Daddy says we'll never give that back, and not just because the Jordanians used stones from Jewish cemeteries there for building things like toilets. It's our "eternal capital." I've never seen Daddy acting so Jewish.

The kids sat up talking very late. They persuaded me to read them this journal, I mean the parts about the war. I skipped the bits about Ofer. I felt myself blushing and Esther noticed and asked me afterward what I missed out. I wouldn't tell her, of course. I do like Ofer, even though he's only two months older than me.

Then we talked about how wonderful it will be to have peace at last, not to be afraid anymore, and for our boys—the ones in our class—not to have to go and fight when they're eighteen. Ofer says he simply can't imagine himself fighting, but then he can't imagine Adam fighting either. Adam is the most gentle, peaceful guy, all he cares about is his archaeology and his cows (he's Dad's boss in the *refet*). And his music . . . Ofer says just the *noise* of battle must have been agony for Adam. His ears are so sensitive he jumps if you shout near him.

Baruch listened to us all talking about peace, not saying much for once. Finally someone couldn't resist—I mean how can anyone be a pessimist *now*?—and said, *"Nu,* say something gloomy," and Baruch said, "What makes you all so sure the Arabs will know they're beaten?" We all hooted. How could they not know they're beaten after this?

I had some private thoughts. First I thought about if Noah will go back to Canada now. Something Mom said made me think she and Dad think Noah and Donna have broken up. I'm almost sure they haven't, and I wish Noah would say something so they don't get too hopeful about him just staying here forever without her.

The other thought I had is that when peace comes, maybe they'll mend the bridge and take away the barbed wire and I'll be able to walk across it and visit with Mustapha and Eeyore. Great, or what? Danny's dad told us, when there's peace, Jordan won't be so poor anymore because we can work together with them, share "expertise" on farming and industry, and anyhow none of our countries will be spending all our money on defense anymore, so we'll all be richer.

And we'll be able to visit Cairo and Damascus and Amman and Beirut! Things are going to be just fantastically wonderful from now on.

T W E N T Y

After the War

"Abba Asher's wrong," said Shula. "Miracles don't come from God. You must to buy them. They are very, very expensive."

She was crying again. In a kibbutz, Lesley'd discovered, you didn't just cry for your own family, because in a sense the whole kibbutz was your family. Shula was crying for Brosh, and for Amnon's brother Yuval, who had died after the "impossible" assault up the Golan Heights into the Syrian guns.

And, perhaps even more than for the others, because it seemed so unbelievable, for their old boss, Moshe the gardener. He would never scold them anymore. He had been shot by a sniper in the Old City, as the victorious

Israelis fought their way through the narrow alleys toward the Wall.

But Rami was safe.

He came home and Shula dried her tears and dragged him to the *kitta,* where they all sat around in the classroom and made him tell them about the war. He told how the Israeli commanders had decided not to shell over the Old City outer walls. It might have broken the Jordanian resistance sooner, and saved lives. But the holy places might have been destroyed—not only Jewish, but Muslim and Christian. Maybe Moshe would have returned, to fret over his ruined lawns and then to restore them, if the Israelis had been prepared to risk the Mosque of Omar, the Holy Sepulcher, the Via Dolorosa where Christ walked to Calvary, and the last precious wall of their own Temple.

Rami described how some of the older men, the officers and army rabbis, when they stood by the Wall at last, had suddenly begun hitting their heads on the stones, rocking and praying and crying and holding up their hands. . . .

"I felt like laughing at first. It looked so weird! But then I looked around at my own bunch, standing there filthy and sweaty and bloodstained with their guns in their hands, and when the old fellow blew the *shofar,* some of them began to cry, too. I felt almost like crying myself, but not from religious feeling. We'd lost so many men getting to it, and now here it was, stuck away in a dirty little alley, looking just like a lot of big stones one on top of another. It made me angry. I'd seen Moshe fall an hour before, and I thought: Are all those stupid stones worth one finger of his hands that could make things grow? His wife won't think so! But now I don't know. I saw those faces . . . and here at home, and in the press, everyone's so excited. . . . I just don't know. Maybe they're more than just stones. Personally I think it wasn't worth a single death, but I have to consider it's just possible that things that last for generations and carry such a deep meaning could be worth more than individual human lives."

Others had their stories to tell, too, and they found eager listeners. But some, like Ofer's brother Adam, wouldn't talk about it.

"Don't ask me," he said to his family. "War just makes me sick. I've got to forget it."

And he went back to the *refet* and hardly talked to anyone about anything for weeks. But just once, when he and Ofer were alone, he suddenly said, "Try not to be in the front line if your turn comes. There's plenty that's useful to do in the rear. Nothing's worth having to kill people for."

And when Ofer, burning with enthusiasm for his brother and the whole army, asked in a shocked voice if saving Israel wasn't worth it, Adam replied, full of bitterness and anger, "Maybe if you're brought up to hate your enemy. Maybe if you're taught to be tough and to block off thinking and feeling. I just couldn't hate enough. It's the kibbutz's fault! They teach us to be human beings and to respect life and not to hate, and then at twenty we're expected to turn around and be ruthless killers."

After this conversation, Ofer lay awake night after night, arguing it out with himself. Lesley sometimes forced herself to stay awake to give him someone to talk to.

200

"He's right. Even now I don't hate them. Even seeing Yocheved crying doesn't make me *hate* them. Just think of putting a bullet into a man, seeing him lying there, knowing you've ended him! I don't know what I'll do when it's my turn. I don't think I can do it."

But surely there would be no need for Ofer's turn ever to come?

All through the long hot months, that summer of 1967, there was hope and jubilation in the air. Now at last, without doubt, the Arabs must sit down around a table and talk to the Israelis face to face, settle everything, make peace. The refugees would be compensated or taken back, the prisoners of war would all be sent home, the borders would be opened, the conquered territories would be returned. Peace, wonderful, longed-for, dreamed-of peace would surely come!

But it didn't. At Khartoum, the Arab nations held a conference and said no. They said it three times: No to negotiations, no to recognition of Israel, no to peace. And slowly, slowly, that feeling of joy and triumph died. The conquered territory stayed conquered, and the Israelis found out that conquest could have a bitter taste for the victors as well.

Shula wrote another English poem, which summed up a lot of people's feelings when it appeared in the kibbutz magazine:

> War . . .
> What that really meant

I never knew.
I don't even know it now.
I never felt a bullet in my body,
And I hope I never will.
I'd never heard the ugly sound of weapons,
Nor feared that someone won't come back.
But what I felt, I can't forget:
Israel is one family, caring for her every son.
I saw all the people so friendly,
No one hated each other, but hated
Something worth hating: the War!
I knew Israel's family well.
The women: waiting, hoping, rushing to every place,
At night alone in a big bed.
No sleep.
But thinking, waiting, hoping.
The children: with confusion, something strange was
    happening.
They knew later, if not then,
Why Mummy loved more, why everyone was so sweet
    to you. . . .
I hardly knew the men. Serious, hard,
Fighting for Israel's family,
Cheering everybody up,
And needing it for themselves.
But I knew the boys, the girls—myself:
Grown in one night, helping the women, smiling
To the men, and laughing with the children.
At night, no light, only candles,
Writing to a soldier-father, a long long letter

202

With jokes.
I knew the Israel family well,
But not the meaning of War.

Lesley had a wise word for Shula, too.

"War's a kind of black magic. It makes some people disappear from the world, it changes others forever. And then, just sometimes, it works good spells, like bringing people together."

She had arrived at this because of the way being together in the war had helped heal the wounds in her family. Things were not quite smooth, there were still scars and unspoken thoughts—but they were together. The question hanging between them now was: Would Noah go back? Or would he stay with them?

Lesley was part of her group now, without doubts or reservations. The bridge business had not initiated her as completely as the war had. During the war she had learned to work as well as any of them; she had proved herself staunch and loyal. Her Hebrew had improved. When Meir came back safe, it was Lesley who was chosen to make a little stumbling speech of love and welcome at the party they gave for him (and it was her mother who baked him a superb cake).

School was out. Working instead was a bore in a way— for Lesley it was the chickens again—but work began at five-thirty, so by ten in the morning she could be at the pool. All the gang came there as they finished work, and they would lie around on the lawns chatting, staring up at the hot blue sky, listening to the joyful racket around them, and plunging into the electric-blue water when they felt too hot. Lesley was chestnut-brown, and her swimming and diving had improved wondrously. As Shula said, quoting her Dad, "Not such a bad old life!" And all the sweeter for thinking what could have happened . . . how they could all have been dead . . .

Noah was lifeguarding again. He didn't mind it quite so much now the war was over, but Lesley could see he was restive.

"I've got no place here," he said. "I'm part of it and yet I'm not. Work and family, that's what gives you your place."

Lesley knew he didn't mean his given family, her and his parents. He meant his chosen family, and that meant Donna.

"What does she say?" Lesley asked. Noah was reading a letter from her.

He heaved a sigh. "That she misses me. That now the war's well over she can't understand why I don't come back. That it makes her mad sometimes. That she worries that I love Israel more than her."

"Does she really say all that?"

"No. She writes about things going wrong with the apartment and the questions our friends ask about me and the stuff in the papers about the Middle East. And she signs it 'Love always no matter what.' "

"And what do you write her?"

"That I want to live in Israel but not in a kibbutz. I'm an engineer, not a farmer, or a lifeguard. I think she likes to hear

that, that everything about her 'rival' isn't perfect. That I get
fed up sometimes, too, and miss her. God, I miss her."

"So go back."

"Trying to get rid of me?"

"I guess I want you to do what's right. It just can't be
right to leave her."

"If only she'd come here!" he burst out.

"Have you asked her?"

"It'd be no use. She's got no ties to this place. And she's
a nurse. She'd have to requalify. That's a lot to ask. She'd
have to want to come."

"Why couldn't it be that she wants to come to be with
you?"

"I 'wanted' to become a Catholic to be with her. I did
it. I lived a lie for years. It didn't work. And she knew it
all the time. I can't ask her to do something like that, to
leave everything she knows just because of my *meshuggass*.
I love her too much."

"Then it's deadlock."

"Yep."

After a pause she began again. "So what'll you do?"

Suddenly he barked.

"I told you, *I don't know*. Oh, go take a jump in the pool,
will you? *Nudnik!*"

And then one day Noah came to the *kitta* while she was
having her siesta. He shook her awake and said, "Come
outside, sis, will you."

She blundered out into the post-noon heat. He was
sitting beside the fish pond with a cable in his hand.

"It's from Donna." He frowned. "It's from Donna," he said again.

"*Nu,* it's from Donna! So tell me!"

"She's going to have our baby."

"*Ya-va-yay!*" breathed Lesley.

"So no more deadlock," said Noah. "That settles it."

"Are you pleased?"

"Years we've been trying. We'd almost given up." He turned to face her, sitting on the grass. They gazed at each other. In his face she saw that he was only at the beginning of taking it in. It was as if the sun was just coming up in his eyes. "You bet your sweet sisterly ass I'm pleased!" he almost yelled.

"Hey, I'll be an aunt!"

They suddenly hugged each other.

"Yeah, but what are the parents going to say?" she asked.

That sobered them fast.

"I dunno. Let's go tell 'em right now before I have time to think about it."

It would be wrong to say that Nat and Miriam had wanted, expected, that the separation between Noah and Donna was permanent. But they had never even met her, never reckoned her in any way as part of the family. They had their son again, and then the war had taken up all their spare thoughts, and somehow neither of them had faced the fact that Noah was still firmly married.

The news of the baby knocked them off balance. They knew at once what it meant. Noah would leave them. And there were evidently no doubts in their minds about the rightness of that.

"New life is the great exception-maker," said Nat slowly, when the first shock had sunk in. "Everything and everybody else comes second to it. Isn't that right, sweetheart?" he said to his wife very gently.

Miriam was sitting quite straight in her chair, staring ahead like a wax figure. "Yes," she said without hesitation, but faintly.

"Mom—"

"No," she said. "Please don't say anything. If you want to be kind, go as quickly as you can."

"Mom, it'll be your grandchild."

She turned to him then.

"Maybe it will," she said. "And then again, maybe it won't. All I know is, it's costing me my son."

"That's no way to look at it, Miriam!" Nat said. "It's not the baby's fault!"

She sighed and hung her head. "I know that," she said. "But it's not real to me yet, and this—this is." She put her hand up to her eyes sharply.

Noah bent over her.

"Mom, it's not forever."

"Don't give me hope," she said. "It's sometimes easier without it."

TWENTY-ONE

Birthday Outing

It was nearly the end of August: nearly Lesley's fifteenth birthday.

As she looked forward to it, she occasionally flashed back to her fourteenth birthday, last summer in Saskatoon. That had hit what she then thought of as an all-time high. Expensive presents, a huge party in a marquee on their lawn all decorated with bought-in flowers, catered food of the most delectable kind, a band, everyone gussied up to the nines . . . The *Star-Phoenix* had printed photos; everyone had talked about it for weeks. Now the memory somehow had power to shame her. It was so showy, so lavish . . . unreal. Too much. Too much of everything. A birthday here in the kibbutz would be a million times better.

More especially because it was to be a very exciting day. It so happened that on it her class was to make a tour of the newly captured part of the West Bank, climaxing with a visit to the Old City of Jerusalem.

It was her good luck, she felt, that the class trip to the Golan Heights was over. That had been more like a journey through hell than a birthday treat.

Bleak, scorched, war-scarred—miles of hot, barren road with nothing worth looking at—stops every now and then to scramble about in fearsome warrens of trenches and concrete bunkers, through the gun slits of which you could look down onto the green valley and the tiny toylike kibbutzim, with their fishponds like dollhouse mirrors. Thus for a generation had the Syrian gunners looked down through their gunsights at their targets below.

There was hardly a sign up there of normal life. No human beings, no houses, only deserted army barracks and blackened ruins. No farming, just weeds and scrubland—a country given over to war.

In the midst of all that desolation, they'd found what must once have been a field, with some tomatoes growing half-wild on their weed-choked, broken stalks. Their suggestive red was the only color in all that dreary landscape. They'd picked some and eaten them, hot and squashy as they were, but their salty-sweet taste made Lesley feel sick. She'd thrown hers away.

The group had grown quieter and quieter. They hadn't recovered their normal spirits until, after hours of bumping along in the back of the truck, they'd descended again into the green richness of Israeli fields and were able to plunge into the Sea of Galilee for a swim.

What bliss—what a relief for body and spirit! They'd shouted and screamed and played wildly, feeling the hopeless sadness of death and defeat, picked up in the very air of the Heights from the departed Syrians, wash off them in their beloved lake.

But this time would be different.

Now they'd see famous old historic towns on the West Bank, and be shown the scenes of battles in which some of their own men had taken part. And at the end—Jerusalem the Golden! No longer divided but reunited. The ancient alleys, the market, the great Walls of Suleiman and the famous gates. The Tower of David, and the Western Wall of the Temple itself. They would see it all. A birthday treat to remember always, a day lifted from among ordinary days, a day when nothing could go wrong.

Early on the morning of her birthday, Lesley woke up to find a tray on the floor beside her bed.

On it were eighteen little plastic bags full of candies, chewing gum, nuts, and breadsticks. Each bag had the name of one of the group on it.

She looked up to see Shula, in the opposite bed, staring at the tray with her mouth open.

"Your parents give you *saciot*? But that's only for little kids!"

Lesley picked up the envelope leaning against the bags.

Darling daughter,

You missed out on all the fun of being a kibbutz child when you were little. We've decided to give you saciot *just once before you have completely grown up.*

We hope this birthday marks the end of your settling in, the beginning of true belonging. We are infinitely proud of you and of the way you've adjusted to our new life. Forgive us if we hurt you or failed to be understanding. We love you so much. We only hope you know, now, that everything that's happened this past year has happened in the framework of that love.

Mazal tov, *Les,*
from Mom and Daddy

If Lesley had felt a trace of embarrassment at the *saciot*, it was soon dispelled. She solemnly gave them out, just as the little kids did on their birthdays, so that all their group would feel part of the celebration, and the others fell into the spirit of the thing at once. There were whoops of delight as they all tucked into the goodies, and fooled around, pretending to be toddlers. Shula disappeared and came back with a towel wrapped around her like a diaper, sucking a lollypop from her *sacit*. Aviva choked on her breadstick and pretended to throw up. Amnon howled for more candy, and Baruch and Gadi had a peanut battle.

Under the empty tray, Lesley found her present from her parents. It wasn't anything like the usual enormous boxes with the old store's name on them. No fancy clothes, figure skates, or Ping-Pong table this year! It was a plain flat packet that could only be an LP record.

211

The others clustered around while she tore off the paper, and then burst into cries of approval.

"Look what she's got!"

"What parents!"

"Eze yofi!"

"Fantasti!"

"Lo normali!"

It was a record of the music of *Hair,* the London production—something they'd all been longing for. But there was no time to play it then. Adda was calling them to get dressed quickly and get out to the truck, which was waiting to take them on the first lap of the Big Trip.

They wore their coolest clothes: shorts, little striped T-shirts with scooped backs and necks, idiot hats pulled well down to shade their faces, and Japanese sandals. As they all climbed the short ladders onto the back of the truck, Adda handed up a bundle of long-sleeved shirts.

"We won't need these! We'll roast!"

"It'll be cool in Jerusalem in the evening. Besides, the Arabs don't like it when you show too much skin."

" 'The Arabs don't like'! Who cares?" asked Amnon loudly.

"Put them under the seats," said Adda sharply. She seemed rather tense, and when she was like this it was best not to argue.

The truck had four rows of hard, narrow bench seats inside, running from front to back, and canvas sides that could be rolled up. You had to decide whether it was more important to get a cool breeze, together with all the dust, or die of heat but keep the air clean. The cool-air people usually won. Ofer, Yossi, and Danny were already rolling up the canvas on their side.

Adda reappeared with boxloads of food and was greeted with a cheer and eager hands. They were already munching their pre-breakfast of bread and gerkins. Churns of cold lemonade were stored up near the cab.

They settled down and sat waiting impatiently for the driver. They gave him the slow handclap, and after a while he and Boaz, who was to accompany them, came strolling out from behind the kitchen, eating sandwiches, and another cheer went up. Boaz jumped in the back with them and pulled up the tailboard, while the driver, who was not a kibbutznik, climbed into the cab.

They were on their way.

The first part of the journey was short. They followed the river south, passed an army roadblock, and were soon driving through what had, until recently, been Jordanian territory.

One could see the difference. No kibbutzim here, of course, no big fields and great blocks of fruit trees, no communal outbuildings and cowsheds. Here were the little jumbled villages made of natural stone or adobe, with just a few grapevines and fig trees in the small yards where the poultry ran loose and a couple of cows were housed in individual sheds, often made of mud brick and roofed with corrugated iron.

The plots of land were small, like patchwork quilts, the furrows running every which way. Even the vineyards were broken up into plots, divided by rough walls made by

213

piling up the stones cleared from the fields. There was no modern irrigation here, but big white wells, like window-less houses, with troughs running around them to water the animals. You saw a few tractors, but mainly it was donkeys, horses, and even an occasional camel. Lesley knew that a lot of the plowing was still done by hand with the ancient biblical type of hand-cut wooden plow.

There was something very beautiful, she thought, about this land and its villages. She even thought "peaceful."

But it wasn't entirely.

Little saucer-eyed children ran out to watch them pass—and were often dragged indoors again by scared-looking women in long, full dresses, with white muslin scarves over their heads.

That was a rather subtle sign of the war. And there were others, if you looked carefully. Here and there a house stood empty, but not yet neglected—as if the households had only just fled. As they travelled deeper into Samaria, they saw more obvious signs: burned-out trucks by the roadside, a freshly ruined house. . . . But for the most part, Lesley was relieved to see that the fields were being worked, and that the people in the villages seemed to be carrying on normally. There were very few soldiers to be seen.

The first town they stopped at was Jenin. Boaz had fought here.

Boaz was a phlegmatic person. The war hadn't bothered him as it had people like Adam. To him it was a job to do. He told even some funny stories: for instance, about when his platoon was winkling out snipers from some houses. Boaz had kicked down a door of one house where they thought there'd been shooting, and burst in—caught sight of a movement—spun around with his Uzi already firing like mad. Then he'd stopped, confused, and heard all his men laughing. He'd been shooting a big mirror to pieces! It was his own reflection he'd seen moving.

The town had a strange feel about it. It was so different from Jewish towns: it was like something out of the past. Nobody wore Western dress. The architecture, the shops, the streets, the people—everything was different. Even the smells. The smells were of animals and spices and strange tobacco and dust, and exotic, wonderful coffee.

They went for a walk in a group and looked at the shops and stalls, sticking to each other like a swarm of bees. Nobody bought anything, though to their astonishment there were dozens of street traders smiling and bowing, obviously anxious to sell to them.

A little boy of about eight ran up to them with a tray of pencils, crying in Hebrew, *"Hacol b'lira! Hacol b'lira!"* They grinned sheepishly at him and shook their heads.

"A lira for a pencil, what a nerve!" whispered David, but Shula said, "That's probably all the Hebrew they've had time to learn."

Lesley thought it odd that these people seemed so friendly, but Boaz said cynically, "Typical. All smiles when they smell money."

"And we Jews don't like doing business?" asked Adda, in the same sharp tone she had used about the shirts.

"They're different. Look at those faces. No, the hatred isn't really forgotten, just pushed behind the come-and-buy smiles till we've gone."

Lesley wished he wouldn't talk like that. She felt sorry

215

for them. It must be awful to have been defeated, and have the conquerors walking about your town staring at you.

The exhilaration, the nervousness, the exciting food smells made them hungry. As they drove to the next place, Adda began to hand around food in packages. There were thick egg sandwiches and pickles and chunks of cold roast chicken wrapped in waxed paper. The driver had to stop in the middle of nowhere, while they took turns to dip into the churns and fill the paper cups with *mitz limon,* which was still deliciously cold.

Some of the boys jumped off the back of the truck to look around, and there was a plea to be allowed to picnic by the roadside, but Boaz wouldn't agree.

"But there's no one around except those field workers way over there," objected Amnon.

"You can't trust them," said Boaz. "Come on, *chevrai,* move!"

Reluctantly the boys scrambled back. The truck was about to start.

Suddenly Adda let out a cry. They all jumped, thinking something had happened.

"Amnon! Yossi! Gadi!" Her voice was like pistol shots. She pointed at the ground behind the truck. "Get out at once and pick up those papers!"

They looked blankly at her, at the food papers left crumpled up on the verge, and finally at each other.

"What's with you?" grumbled Gadi. "It's only rubbish. I thought we'd *done* something."

"You have done something, you little pigs!"

The children gasped. Adda never called them names.

"Where do you think you are? Make a pigsty of your

own place if you like, it's only me that'll have to clear up after you. You're not to leave your mess all over other people's land! Isn't it enough we've beaten them?" Then, as no one moved, she appealed to Boaz. "Tell them!"

Boaz looked sheepish. Clearly he saw nothing wrong with a bit of rubbish, but Adda was glaring at him. He stuck his hands into his pockets and gave a brief nod to the boys. "Better pick it up, *chevrai*," he muttered.

Very unwillingly, Gadi and Yossi climbed down again and picked up their balls of paper, tossing them rebelliously into the back of the truck. Amnon stayed where he was, a look of mulishness settling on his large, red face.

"Are *they* so clean?" he asked.

"That's not the point!" said Adda. "This place is *theirs*!"

"Not anymore," said Boaz unexpectedly.

Adda gave him a look of astonishment and—almost— dislike. The whole group was abruptly stiff with tension and anger. Suddenly they all burst into argument.

"That's right, we won it. It's ours now, we can do what we like."

"No we can't. We'll be giving it back soon, when there's peace."

"*If*, you mean! Anyway, we won't give this part back."

"Of course we will! It's not ours. These people live here. Think how you'd feel, if—"

"I don't have to think how I'd feel!" said Baruch. "I felt plenty when they were threatening to pave the roads with our skulls."

"That wasn't *them*, these farmers, that was their crazy leaders!"

"I bet they loved to hear it, though!"

"Anyway, it doesn't matter if we give it back in the end, we don't have to go throwing litter over it. That's a shame anywhere."

"Yes, we should behave properly and not as if we didn't respect them."

"I don't respect them!" Amnon shouted. "Bunch of murderers!" He was thinking of his brother, and this silenced everyone for a moment.

"As for 'behaving properly,' as you call it," said Baruch slowly, "I just ask myself how 'properly' they'd be behaving if *they'd* won. Never mind a bit of litter. *We'd* be the litter—our corpses."

That did it.

"He's right!"

"They'd have killed the lot of us!"

"Why do we have to be so particular?"

And with that, first Gadi and Yossi, and then one or two more, and finally most of the class screwed up their lunch papers, and started flinging them out all over the road and the ditch. Some flew right into the vineyard beyond. For a few moments, the air was full of flying balls of paper like a fantastic midsummer snowball fight.

Only a few of the girls didn't throw. And Ofer. Ofer was going to—Lesley saw him just raising his arm—but something made her catch hold of his wrist. When he looked down at her, she just begged him with her eyes to be different, not to go with the crowd, and after a moment he shook off her hand and turned away.

After this orgy of littering, there was a sudden silence. They all stood in the truck, looking out at the papers scattered everywhere. They couldn't help seeing how bad it looked. But they were too stubborn to do anything.

"Nu," said Boaz, stirring uneasily. "Let's go."

"Please wait a moment."

It was Adda. Very quietly she pushed through the crowd of children standing between the long benches. Those she brushed past felt how she trembled, and moved aside for her. She climbed backward down the iron ladder, and without a word began picking up the paper balls.

They watched her in shocked silence.

All at once, Ofer nudged Lesley and pointed with his head toward the vineyard. The Arab workers had stopped picking grapes and were standing in a tight group, looking at them.

As Adda, oblivious, crossed the dry ditch and entered the rows of low vines to pick off two balls of paper that had been caught in the leaves, Lesley was horrified to see the group start moving rather quickly toward them.

TWENTY-TWO

A Strange Encounter

The leader was a big Arab in a white head-dress. His dark face was darker still from the scowl on it. His fists were doubled up, and the others, both men and women, about ten of them altogether, came striding along behind him. He had something in his hand that glittered in the sharp sunlight.

He suddenly barked something in a deep, nasal voice, and waved his fist.

At the same moment Lesley screamed out, "Adda! Come back!"

Boaz's head came up like a stag's and he leaped off the tailboard, jumped the ditch, and grabbed Adda, pushing her behind him. She got such a fright that she almost fell, and all the papers she'd been holding spilled onto the ground again.

"Get back in the truck!" Boaz ordered her—and it was an order. He stood facing the oncoming Arabs to cover her retreat. But she didn't retreat at once. Her hands now visibly shaking, she doggedly began picking up all the papers again.

But she kept dropping them.

Finally Lesley simply couldn't stand it. She couldn't. She jumped down and ran to help her, picking up the balls so fast they were just blurs, and then almost dragged Adda back across the ditch, her heart pounding with some unnamable fear.

Boaz and the big Arab were now shouting at each other, in Hebrew and Arabic. Neither understood the other, but the children understood. The Arab was telling them to clear off and leave them in peace, and Boaz was trying to explain, but he was being very aggressive about it, not polite at all. The Arab's voice rose higher and higher, and suddenly he raised his hand menacingly.

"Look out, he's got a gun!" cried Lesley, just like in a film. But Baruch said, "Don't be silly, it's only clippers." And Lesley saw, sure enough, he was holding a pair of grape cutters. But even grape cutters could wound. . . . They watched breathlessly. How could Boaz get out of it without seeming to back down? Should they go and help him somehow?

But just as they thought the tension couldn't be screwed up any tighter, a quiet voice spoke from the driver's cab.

221

"Dai kvar," said the driver's voice. "Enough. Get back. Boaz, let's go."

The big Arab looked toward him and lowered his hand. Grumbling, he backed off, the others behind him backing, too. Boaz, after one glance at the driver, turned and walked calmly back to the truck.

Danny, who'd been craning through the open side, drew his head back in.

"What happened?" asked several hushed voices as the truck jerked forward.

"He's got a rifle," he replied in an awed whisper. "I could just see the barrel sticking out of the window."

They all found seats and huddled into them, sitting close together. Lesley sat next to Adda, who was shaking all over, whether from fear or anger she couldn't be sure. She still had hold of Lesley's hand, and with the other clutched some of the paper balls. Her face was sweating.

Shula raked toward her the empty box the sandwiches had been in, and gently took all the paper balls Lesley and Adda were holding, and put them in. Then she kicked the box under the seat.

The boys were all looking stubborn and defiant, a sure sign that they were feeling like zeroes.

There was very little talking till their next stop, which was Tubas.

"You heard about here," said Boaz. "This was where the people flocked into the streets when we drove through, to welcome us—or so we thought. We were surprised, they seemed so glad to see us! We paraded through the town in our tanks and half-tracks, there were flags every-where, and the folks were all cheering. . . . And then all of a sudden the cheering died and the flags vanished and in two minutes the streets were empty and all the shutters were going up."

"Why? Why? What happened?"

"They'd been told the Iraqis were coming!"

Everyone laughed and felt easier.

In Tubas it was market day. The town was alive with bustle and trade, and there were a few Israeli soldiers lounging about looking bored, so the group decided they might be bold enough to go a little farther from the truck and perhaps even buy a souvenir or so, to take home.

There wasn't much worth buying. There were stalls full of junk, mostly made in Hong Kong, little tinny toys and every sort of plastic horror. But finally they found a shop that sold Hebron glass, and several of them bought the beautiful irregular beads and medallions and little vases in yellow, peacock blue, or green, hand-blown and full of tiny bubbles. The shopkeeper seemed genuinely friendly and insisted on bringing out coffee for them in tiny cups on a round brass tray.

The bee swarm cautiously broke up into smaller clumps. Lesley's group, which included Ofer, Shula, and Esther, strolled along the main street (which they'd been told not to leave) watching the bright bustle of the market. Lesley was thinking how strange it was: all these people who, such a short time ago, had been their enemies, now smiling and beckoning to them, the age-old craving for trade pushing enmity aside. It was a good thing anyway. Trading was

223

obviously better than fighting. And if they still held some hatred in their hearts, well, could you blame them? Could there be a better cure for it than doing business, which the Jews enjoyed as much as themselves? Adda was quite right about that.

"Hacol b'lira! Hacol b'lira!"

The cry was familiar to them already, and they grinned at each other. "More pencils?" asked Lesley, craning to see where the voice was coming from.

"No, nuts this time—look—almonds! He's over there. Let's get some."

Lesley followed Ofer's pointing finger and saw the street seller, a thin boy half-turned away from them with a tray of small paper pokes of shelled almonds hung around his neck.

"Hacol b'lira!"

"A lira per nut, no doubt," murmured Esther as they pushed toward him through the crowd.

Just at that moment, the boy turned his black head toward them and Lesley stopped in her tracks, staring in disbelief. And when he saw her, the street cry stuck between his lips.

It was Mustapha.

Lesley had no way of knowing what had been happening to Mustapha since that morning by the river. But a great deal had. He was three months older in time—three years in experience.

Before, he had been a fourteen-year-old boy, his body thin and small through overwork and underfeeding in his childhood, his eyes narrow and dark with depths of hard knowledge of a hard-driven people and their ways of survival.

But now many new things had happened. His father, whom he disliked and feared, had, when the war started, taken him and his eldest sister and fled to the home of his brother, Mustapha's uncle, who lived in Tubas.

It was a foolish thing to do, but Mustapha's father was not a clever man, and just then he was a frightened one as well. All he knew was that Tubas was a lot farther from the Israeli border than their own little village; therefore it seemed safer, even though it was on the western bank of the river.

He would have done better to keep that sluggish, narrow, vital stream between him and the enemy.

He left his wife and five small daughters behind in the village without thinking twice. They were women and hardly counted. He took his eldest daughter because he would need a female to look after him in his brother's house, so as not to have to depend entirely on *his* women.

When the soldiers marched into Tubas, the two brothers were among those who poured out of their barricaded houses to cheer their Iraqi allies—and fled back into them pellmell when they saw the blue-and-white Israeli flags and the star-shaped markings. They cowered indoors, expecting the worst of worsts, and only days later, when food was running short, did they send their womenfolk out to see if the market was functioning and if the enemy had moved on. They found that the leaders of the town had long since surrendered.

225

Mustapha had watched all this with his wise little face blank, his narrow, observant eyes unreadable. Only once, to his big sister, did he open his mouth.

"Our father is a fool and a coward."

She recoiled at this disrespect.

"How can you speak so? Our father is our father!"

"You don't know. I can see what's true. He curses our army, but what did *he* do? He ran like a jackrabbit. If only I was old enough! How I would fight them! How I would kill, kill, kill them and drive them back into the sea!"

He pounded the tiled floor with his fist, bruising his hand and making the loose bits of cement jump. His sister watched him with a blank black look like his own, but with a bit of feminine slyness in it.

"Would you kill also the Jew girl whose picture you keep in your shirt?"

Mustapha's head came up, and the next minute he was on his feet and going for her, but she was a big strong girl and she pushed him away with one flat blow of her hand.

"Don't talk so much of killing till you get some strength in your body, little brother," she sneered, hands on hips, above him as he sprawled on the floor.

"Pig's daughter, I will kill *you*!" he shouted, and came at her again, but she quickly dodged from the room and bolted the door behind her, taunting him through it, "Will you? Come and try, little donkey! I'll ride you to market!"

His sister wouldn't have dared treat him like that in front of their father, but he was out at the café drinking coffee and smoking his *nargileh* as usual, and Mustapha was left with nothing to do but kick the door till his foot ached, and

226

then go out to the yard and console himself with his donkey.

Once he would have gone out and beaten it to relieve his feelings, but things were different now. When he had seen Lesley fondling and petting it, he had been amazed. To be friends with an animal! To give it tidbits and talk to it! —Until that time he would as soon have thought of patting and talking to a plow.

He felt foolish at first when he began to stroke and speak to the donkey, and made very sure nobody saw him. But it was strange how it changed him. He had no brothers. A few friends he had, in the village, but they all worked as hard as himself and there wasn't much time for playing or talking together. The donkey spent all day with him. It was warm and soft. It responded to his touch and his voice, and was never sly or cruel or indifferent like some of the humans around him.

And a funny thing happened. When his mother saw that he was beginning to be fond of the beast, she didn't laugh. She gave him leftover carrot tops, or spoiled cabbage leaves, or sometimes even bruised fruit to give to his "friend." His softening toward the donkey softened her toward him.

It didn't soften his father, though. To see him beating the donkey now made Mustapha feel sick with anger—and shame, for he hated to be reminded how he had once treated it himself.

Now he sat in the dirty straw by the donkey's front feet, and it put its gray nose down to be rubbed. Mustapha felt so churned up that he would have cried, if he had not long ago got over crying.

He sat there cursing his father, his sister, the Israelis, the Arab armies who had been defeated and left him with this burning sense of shame. The donkey meanwhile nibbled his ear with its rubbery lips, and after a little while he couldn't help laughing because it tickled.

"Donkey, donkey, donkey," he said in a singsong voice.

He lay down on his back and played with the soft gray head that nudged at him.

"When I'm grown, I shall join Al Fatah. Properly, not just doing odd jobs to borrow the binoculars. I shall learn to fight like ten lions. I shall be the bravest fighter of them all. I shan't have to cross the river now to lay my mines and plant my bombs—I can do it right here, for the enemy is here, strolling around the town, sneering at us . . . while our people serve them and smile, but only because we know we shall kill them all one day. . . ."

Was it true? Or was he alone in his determination for revenge?

He thought of his father and uncle, gloating between customers at his uncle's grocery shop.

"Business has never been better! These Jews know how to buy."

"Perhaps as time passes, we can sell our goods across the line. Fruit—nuts—other things. The young fellows can offer their labor—the Jews are building, always building, and they'll need workers in other trades. The war may have been no bad thing in the end."

"If only there's no more trouble! We may all make some real money out of these people."

They even fawned on the soldiers. It seemed to Mustapha that just by entering the shop with money in his

228

pocket, any creature could become a friend and an equal in the eyes of his father and his uncle.

Now they'd left their land, they were not farmers anymore. They had to earn another way, a way of humiliation to Mustapha. He was ordered into the streets, to be shoved and jostled, to peddle his nuts to anyone willing to buy. Those nuts were something even the poorest Jew could afford. He sold more to them than to the townspeople.

But that didn't mean he had to smile at them. When they bought, he stared into their eyes with a blank look that just masked his hatred. He would not let his hands touch theirs, even to take money. He obliged them to put their dirty coins onto his tray and take the nuts without his help. It was the only gesture left to him, but it made him feel a little less ashamed, a little less defeated.

And he dreamed. Not just daydreams. Asleep, he often dreamed of the river. Once he had crossed it, with others, buoyed up with comradely courage. He had closed his mind to danger and charged across, up the bank, across the wasteland, under the fence, straight to the house he had studied and picked, staring through the borrowed binoculars—the house of the girl's parents.

He had crept in, snatched the few "proofs" he needed, stuffed them in his shirt—then seen the photograph— heard movements within—made instinctively for the screen door, stepped back irresistibly, snatched the photo, out, down the steps in one leap, ran, ran, dived for the fence, up, the ground not touching his feet as he flew toward the river. . . . In his dreams he really flew, high up, a bird, safe from their guns.

But the other dream was worse.

Crouching in the long grass all night in the shadow of the bridge with chattering teeth, the donkey like a gray ghost gone to the land of the dead, and unrecoverable. His back aflame from his father's beating, afraid almost his father would kill him, and yet— Powerless. Unable. Unable to force himself to cross. It was a nightmare he woke from sweating.

But the part that came with the morning, that was all happiness. The meeting knee-deep in the river, the sublime taste of the chocolate, the unnamable relief of laying hands again on his lost beast, and the birth of love in him, though he only realized this vaguely, in the bliss of the dream that was not specific but like a bright morning mist: softness in his hand, sweetness in his mouth and joy in his heart.

Now he stood in the market and stared at the girl, surrounded by others, other Jews, all looking at him, all hateful to him, all except her.

"Mustapha!" she called.

The Jews burst into talk, questions. Beyond *"Hacol b'lira"* he knew none of their cursed language. But he would not retreat. He stood. And after a few moments he saw that she had sent her friends to the other side of the street to wait for her. That she was coming toward him. That they would meet.

A Crumpled Picture

"Salaam."

"Salaam."

They looked at each other, awkward, happy, embarrassed. Then she put out her right hand and he took it and shook it and they half laughed.

"How is your peace?" she asked in Arabic.

"My peace is good. And yours?"

"Also good."

They spoke stiffly, but their eyes were shining. They were each strangely thrilled to see the other. Their meeting seemed to both uncanny, an event not to be dreamed of, like the other—not part of normal life but like a fable.

"What you do here?" she asked. Her Arabic was basic and faulty, but he understood her.

"What you see. Selling. You want nuts?" He took a bag and offered it to her. "No money. I give you. Take it."

She took the little poke made of a scrap of Arabic newspaper and ate a nut, and offered one to him. "Your nuts?" she asked.

"My uncle's."

They ate another nut to cover their awkwardness.

"What are you doing in Tubas?" he asked her.

"Trip with my class."

"You like our country?" he asked with a hint of irony.

She flushed. "Yes. I like the villages. Why you leave your village?"

"The war."

"Oh. Yes. It goes well with you here?"

"Not so good."

"I'm sorry. How's Eeyore?" she suddenly asked eagerly.

"What?"

"Oh . . ." She giggled, and a smile twitched his tough mouth. "The donkey. I call him Eeyore. Hee-haw," she explained.

"He's good."

"You keep your promise?"

"Yes."

"You don't beat him?"

"Only when he's slow." He wasn't going to let her know how completely he had kept his word.

"I said 'never'!" she exclaimed, her eyes flashing.

He didn't answer. His breath was stopped. She was not

like any girl he had ever seen. The way she met his eyes with hers would be shameless boldness in an Arab girl, yet with her it was different, it sent a different signal that he couldn't read. And she seemed to have hardly any clothes on. He badly wanted to touch her bare arm and he dared not glance downward at her legs. He moved a step back.

"This is your work now? The nuts?" she asked. He nodded. "Then you don't need a donkey."

"We need him. We would be nothings without a donkey. He carried all our things from our village. Many kilometer. He never gets tired."

"I think you love him now."

"Of course not. He's just an animal."

They stood in silence for a moment.

"You can't go home now," she suddenly realized.

"No."

"Your mother . . . ?"

He shrugged. He refused to think of her, of his little sisters left to their fate. It made him too angry.

"Do you like . . ." She hesitated. She glanced over her shoulder at her friends, as if measuring them. Then she finished her sentence. "You like to visit our—village?"

"What?"

"Where I live. You like to visit the kibbutz? You can see your village from there."

He was dumbstruck. Suddenly he almost shouted, "No!"

"Why you angry?"

He turned his head away, but not before she had seen the look in his eyes.

233

"I understand how you feel. About us. About the war—"

"No. You can't understand."

"But you—and me—we're not—enemies."

He looked around slowly. His eyes were lustrous like black olives, and just as bitter, but they softened a little as they looked at her.

"Perhaps no. But to all your people I am enemy."

"Don't say that!"

"You want a lie? I tell truth. For now. Forever."

"But the war's over!"

"This war. Not next war. Next war. Next war." His hand gestured into infinity.

"It can't be like that!" she said. "It can't be! You can't want it to. It must stop. We must have peace."

"You can say 'peace,'" he said in a man's voice. "You—won. But when you lose, it is different. You can't think of stopping. You must think only of fighting, till you lose your . . ."

"Your life?"

"No! Till you don't have to feel—" He curled his hand into a hard claw and made a savage gesture toward his chest as if something were tearing at him.

Suddenly understanding, Lesley said in English, "Ashamed."

He said nothing.

"Then it will go on forever. Because someone must always lose."

"It will not be us. Not at the end," he said.

•   •   •

234

Lesley was speechless. If it were true, it was too awful. A deep feeling of horror swelled inside her. A vista of the future—looking like the Golan Heights, pitted with bunkers and graves and nothing growing but little blood-red fruits—spread in her mind's eye.

Suddenly she thought of Noah. He was coming back to them. He had written that Donna had agreed to come, to try it, as soon as the baby was six weeks old. The baby . . . It might be a boy. Like Ofer, like the others, his turn might come. It would come, if Mustapha meant it. Then why should they stay? Why should anyone stay in Israel, or come here, if Mustapha was right?

It came down to him and her. If they could not make peace, then . . .

"But you wouldn't kill me?"

"I don't know," he said. "Perhaps. If I fight your village, and you are killed, I am sorry. But you are just one person. I am just one person. We are not important."

"We are!" she cried out. "We are important!"

"No. My father. He thinks he is important. If you think you are important, you behave like—"

He stopped. He was looking over her shoulder. She turned. Ofer and the others were coming across the street toward them.

Mustapha said distantly, "Your friends are coming. Good-bye." He began to move away from her.

"Mustapha, don't go! Can't we . . . ?"

He stopped and made a sudden movement with his hand into his shirt. He pushed a crumpled, fuzzy piece of paper into her hand.

235

"I don't want this anymore."

Then he was gone.

For several moments she was able to follow his black head until it disappeared around the edge of a stall selling watermelons. She stared, her mind in confusion. Then she looked down.

In her hand, dog-eared, worn, and soiled, was her photograph. Yet its creases had been made by his hand only a moment ago. Till then it had been kept smooth, and the other damage had been caused by much handling.

She stared at it with a hollow sense of loss. It was more than the loss of a friend, or the exchange of a friend for an enemy. It was something like the loss of hope. Her mother had said sometimes things were easier without hope, but that was rubbish. *Shtuyot.*

The others burst to her side through the crowd.

"Nu? What did he say?"

"How long you were talking!"

"What did he give you?"

Lesley tried to pull herself together. "Just some nuts. Here, have some."

"But what did he say?"

"Oh—just some *shtut.* It doesn't matter. Come on, let's get back to the others."

Ofer and Esther led the way back to the truck, but Shula kept Lesley a little way behind.

"It was him, wasn't it? Your boyfriend from across the river."

"Yes."

"What you crying?" she whispered in English.

236

"I'm not!" said Lesley fiercely.

"It wasn't just *shtut,* was it?"

"Yes it was! He's crazy, he can't understand anything! Oh—" Her voice pitched up shrilly. "Stop talking about him! He's an Arab, they're all the same!"

"No," said Shula quietly. "Not right."

Lesley knew it, and she knew that Shula knew she hadn't meant it. You could say awful things sometimes to a real friend. Yet when Shula tried to hold her arm, she drew away. She kept seeing Mustapha's eyes.

TWENTY-FOUR

A Crack
in the Wall

The truck racketed along the road to Jerusalem. The children all sang the latest pop song, which, oddly, was also a sort of hymn that had come out of the war:

"Jerusalem of gold, of copper and light! For all your songs, I'll be the violin. . . ." After a while Lesley sang with the others.

At the Old City, they parked outside the Golden Gate and made straight for the Wall. The religious authorities had already made separate sections for men and women. To the kibbutz children this was a joke, but if you wanted to approach the Wall, there was nothing for it but to accept the new rules. The boys had to cover their heads.

238

Lesley was more interested in the place itself. Rami had said the Wall was in a narrow alley, but this had changed. The Israelis had begun to bulldoze a wide area in front of it to make an open square. The Wall itself now loomed up like a monolith, each stone so huge that it seemed a miracle it could have been lifted and laid.

And into the cracks and crevices between these vast blocks, in obedience to ancient tradition, religious Jews piously slipped bits of paper with prayers written on them. Lesley watched them, the men with their broad-brimmed hats and beards and side curls on the far side of the barrier, "davening" as her father called it—rocking as they intoned their prayers. On her side, the women prayed more restrainedly, swathed in shawls that covered all their hair. They were more alien to her than Mustapha had been.

And only a little distance from the Wall itself, modern life took over. Hundreds of Israelis and tourists in bright summer clothes strolled about, taking photographs, chatting—and buying souvenirs. The sellers, mostly Arabs, were selling souvenir medals of Moshe Dayan and other Israeli heroes. How helpless and degraded they must feel, to have come to that so quickly!

The edge of the cleared part was piled high with broken stones and masonry. Lesley tugged Boaz's arm.

"Did they have to break down homes?"

"Whole streets. No doubt the people were compensated," said Boaz. "The Wall's going to be the center of the Jewish world from now on. Thousands, maybe millions, will want to come here."

Lesley said no more. People had lived here. Perhaps the

very spot she was standing on had been some Arab's living room. It made her feel very uncomfortable. She looked again at the Arabs selling the medals, and others, just beyond the square, with ice-cream stands and stalls for coffee and other food . . . like Mustapha. And like him, probably filled with hatred, with a longing for revenge, for the next war which might bring their shame to an end.

She kept sighing. Her heart was bruised.

When they all walked through the old market to-gether—something she would normally have reveled in, for it was like scenes from the Arabian Nights—she was too depressed to look properly at the myriad delights on every side. Jewelry, rugs, sheepskin coats, beautiful embroidered dresses, huge round trays of honeyed cakes, leather, glass, painted pottery, brass and copper—all slipped past the tails of her eyes in an exotic blur, while the others dashed in all directions with cries of excitement, and Adda and Boaz kept struggling to keep them together, rounding up strag-glers like a pair of sheepdogs.

All the time Lesley's hand was in the pocket of her shorts. In the truck she had had a strong impulse to throw the crumpled photograph angrily away. That had passed. Now her fingers curled around it lightly but tensely, as if protecting it.

All too soon, it was time to start for home. They had explored the market, had coffee and carrot juice (Adda wouldn't let them taste the fly-blown cakes) and bought souvenirs, stood under the great crenellated towers of the Jaffa Gate, touched the sun-whitened stones of King

240

David's Tower, and seen the exquisite Mosque of Omar.

Now they were very tired. It was suddenly almost too much effort to drag their weary feet back to where they had left the truck, outside the City walls, beside the Dome of the Rock. The sun was going down.

Shula was the first to notice.

"Lesley's gone!" she cried fearfully. "She's not with us!"

Adda, who had spent much of the day in a state of dread that something like this would happen, clutched Boaz with one hand and the driver with the other.

"Go! Go find her! Where did you last see her—any of you?"

"In the Mosque! In the market! Near the Tower!"

The two men dashed back through the gates of the Old City. Adda ordered the others to get into the truck, and forbade anyone to get out or wander off. A few pleaded for ice creams from a nearby kiosk, but Adda was too agitated to take the slightest further risk now it was getting dark.

"I knew we couldn't get through the day without *something*!" she kept moaning, wringing her hands. "Oh, where is she?"

Next moment, Ofer, lingering on the tailboard of the truck, gave a shout and pointed to the gate.

It was Lesley. She was running toward them through the strange, mystic, sun-echoing glow of the Jerusalem twilight. Her feet were noiseless as they flew over the cobbles, and her face had a queer limpid look of tranquility.

Adda first hugged her, then chewed her to pieces, while she hung her head and gave no explanation. Then Adda cuffed her behind hard and sent her up into the truck. It was almost dark in there, and while Adda fussed outside about how they could let the men know she was found, Lesley squeezed in at the end of the bench next to Ofer and gazed out over the hills, where a last touch of red-gold sunlight was still to be seen, burning on the far crests.

"Jerusalem of gold, of copper and light," she sang softly to herself.

"Where did you go?" hissed Shula, leaning forward from her place opposite.

"Back to the Wall."

"What for, though?"

But Lesley didn't reply.

Her pocket was empty now. The long-cherished, and rejected, photograph was lodged in a chink as high as she could reach, pushed far in and wedged there with a little stone. On the back of it, under the now unreadable notes written by her mother, was a brief prayer, written in three languages with a stump of pencil she had borrowed from a stranger.

"Peace between us and between our peoples."

Of course, it was superstition really, she supposed. But anything that gave you back a little hope, when you'd nearly lost it, was as good as a miracle.

The two men were found, and they started home. The light faded through pale gilt to pearl, to the star-silvered blackness of a moonless summer night.

Lesley gazed out at it through the square dark frame at the back of the lurching truck. The lights of men and of God twinkled face-to-face across limitless black spaces. The mysteries of war and peace, friend and enemy, love

242

and hatred, were swamped for the time being in that vast star-sandwiched emptiness.

Lesley allowed her heart an hour's peace, and was so rapt in it that she didn't even notice at first that Ofer was holding her hand.

And Mustapha?

Mustapha sat in the straw and leaned his thin back against the thin ribs of his donkey and let the poison of hatred wash out of him, a burning, bitter salt tide of tears.

It was so long since he had cried that he had forgotten the taste. He didn't understand why he cried or why he was suffering. He felt as if peeling the photo away from his side had uncovered a wound that was bleeding.

He wanted it back. He wanted it back! It had been like a talisman, and now he had thrown it away he felt unsure, unsafe. He no longer knew for certain what he was or what he would be. He had said that he was of no importance, that *she* was of no importance, and she had denied the truth of that, and he believed *her* and not himself.

He didn't in the least know why, but his tears, his powerful sense of loss, told him that he and that girl he would never see again were the two most important people in the world.

Glossary of Hebrew and Yiddish Words

abba: father
akhora: backward
aleph: first letter of the alphabet
Arabush: derogatory term for an Arab
Aravim: Arabs
avodat-bayit: homework

baruch ha'ba'a: welcome (literally, blessing to the comer)
beged: garment; plural: **begadim** (clothes)
beged-yam: swimsuit
beseder: okay, all right
bet: second letter of the alphabet
betakh: of course
betakh sh'lo: of course not
bubbalink: love-name

calaniot: anemones
chevrai: "gang," group of kids
communa: communal laundry

dafka: the opposite of what you'd expect
dai: enough
dai kvar!: enough already!

eze yofi!: how lovely!

fleishiker (Yiddish): meaty, a meat meal

gan: kindergarten
gever: attractive man
gimmel: third letter of the alphabet
gvul: border

hacol: all
hacol b'lira!: everything for a lira!
hashka'a: irrigation

ima: mother, mom
Ivrit: Hebrew

kadima: forward
katan: little
kavod: honor
kees: pocket
khamor: donkey
kharar: disgusting substance (swear word)
khasiot: brassieres
khasitot: battle fronts
kibbutznik: kibbutz-dweller
kitta: classroom or classroom-building
kol tuv: good luck
kova: hat
kova tembel: hat shaped like dunce's cap

lahitra'ot: so long, good-bye for now
limon: lemon
lira: unit of Israeli money (now obsolete)
lul: chicken house

246

madrikh: youth leader; feminine: **madrikha**
ma pitom?: what next?
mazal tov: congratulations
mensch (Yiddish): a "macho" man; plural: **menschen**
meshuggah, meshuggat: crazy
meshuggass: madness
metapelet: housemother, children's care-giver
mikasakhat: lawn mower
milchiker (Yiddish): milky, a dairy meal
mishkefot: binoculars, field glasses
mitz: fruit juice
mitbakh: kitchen
mitzvot: righteous deeds, ritual actions
motik: sweetie, honey

noi: landscape gardens
nu?: well?
nudnik: one who talks or nags too much

off: hen

pardess: citrus plantation
pesach: Passover
p'oola: activity, action (often military); plural: **p'oolot**

refet: cowshed, dairy

sabra: native-born Israeli (also: prickly pear)
sacit: a little bag; plural: **saciot**
schmattedic (Yiddish): ragged, old (clothes)
schmattes: rags
seder: order of service for Passover
shabbat: sabbath (Saturday)
shalom: greeting (hello, good-bye); peace
sheket!: quiet!
sheli: my, mine
shofar: ritual ram's horn
shtok!: shut up!